Muddy Waters

Stu Campbell

ISBN: 978-0-9962019-7-1

6   5   4   3   2   1

Edited by Mira Perrizo
Cover and text design by D.K. Luraas
Cover painting by Larry Jones, Bouse, Arizona
Author photo by Joanne Winer

Printed in the United States of America

Contents

1

Letter of Thanks

The trip from the Wilson Ranch back to his cabin was uneventful and Mud was smiling all the way. He had escaped Virginia Abercrombie's clutches successfully and he didn't feel like a thief in the night. He looked forward to tending his garden, looking after his small cowherd, and just watching the wild horses that roamed the area. Mud had led a fairly peaceful life since he'd parted ways with Virginia, although he'd had a few wild times. He'd had a knee problem that was very painful and since the doctors couldn't seem to fix it, he told them, "Either fix it or cut it off! It's really painful and I can't hardly get on my horse."

After an unsuccessful knee replacement, Mud simply told his surgeon to cut it off. So they did. He'd spent some time rehabilitating and getting used to his artificial leg, first on crutches then with a walker and then with a cane. Soon he wasn't using any of the aids. He told his physical therapist, "Even with the pain of the amputation, the daily pain is less now."

Arriving at his place, after they unloaded the horses and Mud's saddle and bedroll, he told Pat, "I do appreciate you bringing me back down here. It would have taken a couple of days horseback. But it'll mean a long day for you by the time you get back."

"That's not a problem, old partner," said Pat. "I'm glad you showed up when you did. If you hadn't, we might still be gathering cattle."

"I don't know that I was much help. That Honey's quite a hand and Rod hasn't forgotton anything about cows even though he's been in the sheep business all these years. That Jimmy is a good hand and I'd expect that knowing how good a hand his dad was, and Sally is as good as anybody. The only thing missing was Bud. If he'd have been there, it would have been like the old days."

"And, of course," said Pat jokingly, "Virginia being there made it more like the old days!"

"Virginia made it very uncomfortable!" retorted Mud.

"I actually thought she made it comical," said Pat.

"Comical! It wasn't funny to me!"

"It was comical to watch you around her," replied Pat. "I never knew you had such a fear of women!"

"If I'd have known she was there, I never would have showed up in the first place!"

"I'm glad you did. We haven't seen you for quite a while and had actually lost track of you. We'd heard something about you having your leg cut off, but didn't know whether to believe it or not. But I'd better be goin', I'm not gettin' any closer to gettin' home standin' around jawing like this."

"Make sure you don't tell Virginia where my place is!" said Mud. "If she showed up, I'd have to leave here and I've sorta got used to it, even like it."

"I won't tell," said Pat. "Your old truck there, does it run?"

"Certainly," replied Mud. "I do have a tough time shifting gears with this artificial leg, but if I ain't goin' too awful fast, I can manage."

"Well, don't be a stranger. Drop by occasionally." With that, they shook hands and Pat shoved an envelope into Mud's hand. "That's from Bud," he said, as he got into the truck. He drove away before Mud could open the envelope and try to return the money that was in it. The money was wages for his help in gathering the cattle.

"That's just like Bud Wilson," said Mud to himself. He counted the money and said, "He's overpaid me for what I did." Still talking to himself, he said, "I ought to return it to him, but it ain't half enough to pay for havin' to put up with Virginia the way I did!"

He put the envelope in his pocket and grained his horses in the corral. While they were eating, he hobbled them and went to the house, leaving the corral gate open. The horses would come in for grain in the morning, but Mud felt more secure hobbling them. They wouldn't be so apt to be run off by the mustang studs and if they were, they wouldn't go far being hobbled.

Winter was approaching and Mud thought about what he had to do to get ready for the cold weather. He had plenty of firewood stacked up and had enough hay put away to feed his horses and cows over the winter. He thought he ought to go to town and get more propane for his heater and more gas for his truck and generator. He had portable propane tanks and jerry cans for the gas.

He'd grown enough vegetables to last him the winter and he could shoot a deer or butcher a calf when he needed meat. Other than the trip to town, he was set. He figured himself to be pretty much self-reliant. He would need to get someone to haul his calves to the sale when the time came, and he'd go to town to watch the sale and get a check.

He thought when he went to town for the propane and gas, he'd get some new clothes with the money Pat gave him. He also thought he'd buy a new radio. He didn't really get good radio reception at his place, and he thought a newer radio might improve the situation. It was the only contact he had with the outside world during the winter. Of course he couldn't call out on the radio, it was just for listening to.

Not being one to waste time making elaborate plans, he decided he'd go the next day. He'd built a tripod with a block and tackle and loaded the propane tanks in the truck. He could lift the jerry cans in by hand. It might be wise to go before the snow came. When the snow did come, he was essentially snowed in for the winter. He thought he ought to send Bud a note of thanks for the money he'd sent with Pat.

That night he wrote a letter to Bud thanking him for the money and telling him he hoped he hadn't got in the way during the roundup. He invited Bud, Pat, Honey, and Sally to come down and visit if they had a chance. He purposely omitted Virginia. He sealed the letter and addressed it and without thinking, put his own mail box number on the envelope as a return address.

The town where he traded was about a hundred miles from the town closest to the Wilson Ranch and about fifty miles from his place. In town the next day, he checked his mail and didn't get anything of importance. He mailed his letter to Bud and went to the sale barn.

At the sale barn he met the manager and told him, "I'll

have about thirty calves to bring to the sale in two weeks, but I need to hire someone to haul them."

"We hauled 'em in last year, Dusty," said the manager. "It took us two trips to get 'em all. We need to get the semi to haul 'em this year. Can a tractor-trailer make it up there? There are some pretty sharp turns on that road."

Mud wasn't accustomed to being called by his given name, Dusty, and was taken back a little to hear it, but he recovered and said, "A big rig can make it before the snow falls. The forest service keeps the roads in pretty good shape until hunting season. I'll have the cattle gathered in by Wednesday if you can have a truck there Thursday. The sale's still on Saturday, isn't it?"

"Yep," said the manager.

"They'll need to be fed and watered good Thursday and Friday night," said Mud.

"That'll be taken care of. We'll need to charge you for the haul."

"That's fine. Just take it out of my check. I'll need to sort the calves from the cows and I could use some help doing that. I don't get around very good with this artificial leg. Be there early, I'll have the cattle corralled."

"We'll be there shortly after sunup, although we'll probably have to charge you overtime for the driver gettin' up early."

"With all this charging for the haul, overtime, and your commission, is there going to be any money left for me?" asked Mud.

The sale manager laughed. "There should be. You want us to send you the check?"

"Nope. I'll be in to get it on Saturday. I want them sold early before all the buyers fill their orders and leave. The prices are better early," said Mud. Mud left the sale yard and went to get his propane tanks and gas cans filled.

With the tanks filled with propane and the jerry cans filled with gas, Mud went to the clothing store and bought some new winter clothes. As he drove back to his place, he thought he'd better be extra careful. Loaded with propane and gas as he was, he laughed as he thought of himself as a portable bomb. *Won't be no laughing matter if I wreck this thing!* he thought.

As far as he knew, he was set for winter. He made a mental note of what he needed and decided to write down a list when he got back to his ranch. He could add a few things if he thought of them and get them when he went to the sale.

At the ranch, he made his list and added a portable battery charger. The next day he unloaded the propane tanks and gas cans. He caught up his horse and went to look after his cattle. If he moved them closer to the corrals, they'd be easier to gather for the sale. As he rode out, he thought he ought to build a fence and make a pasture closer to the ranch so he could make sure the cattle wouldn't wander off.

He didn't like the thought of building fence. It was difficult to dig postholes with his artificial leg. He decided he'd use steel posts and build a suspension fence and use wooden stays to help keep it up.

He found most of his cattle and started herding them toward the ranch. He left the cattle not far from the house, hoping they'd stay close. He rode to the barn, unsaddled his horse, grained him, hobbled him, and turned him loose.

Then he went to the house and added steel posts, barbed wire and staples to his list. He also added a steel post driver to his list. He had a piece of pipe he could use, all he needed to do was have a welder weld a piece of metal to one end and he had it made.

2

Building Fence

The next day he went out on foot and started to dig post-holes for his brace and corner posts. He started at his corrals.

He had plenty of cedar posts available and a partial roll of barbed wire on hand. By noon he had a brace built on the side where he wanted the gate to be. He paced off what he thought would make the side of a forty-acre pasture and decided to go a little farther to include the creek. At the far side of the creek he built a corner brace. Then he went directly to the left, about the same distance, and built another corner brace. He then went to the left again and paced off approximately the same distance and built another corner brace.

He had three corner braces built and he thought if he continued straight, he could connect his new fence to the old one. He'd still have to build one more brace, but he could hang another gate from his brace post. He thought he'd save himself some digging by doing this. The digging was difficult with his artificial leg.

It was getting late and Mud decided to call it a day. He had a long walk back to the house and he still had to fix some supper. On the way, he reminded himself to add another gate to his list. All his gates were swinging gates, as he had difficulty opening and closing wire gates.

The next day, he saddled his horse and went out to check on his cows. He found the cows he'd pushed closer the day before and they hadn't strayed too far, so he went to look for more cows. He found more cattle and his bull and moved them to the others. He got a count on them and decided he'd found all his cattle.

He wished he had the pasture already built. He'd have to ride every day to keep the cattle close so they'd be ready to corral, sort, and load when the truck came. So he rode every day and kept the cattle close. On Thursday morning, before sunup, he was in the saddle gathering his cattle. By the time the truck arrived, he had the cattle corralled and was sorting the calves from the cows.

The truck driver backed the truck up to the loading chute, climbed out and hollered at Mud, "You about ready to go, old timer?"

"Almost," replied Mud. "If you'll work that gate, we'll have 'em right directly."

The driver climbed into the corral and worked the gate according to Mud's directions.

"I want to add a couple of cull cows and the bull. You got room for 'em?"

"We'll make room," said the driver. "Don't you want them other calves?"

"Nope," said Mud. "They're my replacement heifers."

They loaded the calves then loaded the cows in the back compartment of the trailer.

"You make sure they get fed good tonight and tomorrow. I'll be in early Saturday to watch the sale.

The truck pulled out and Mud turned his cows out.

I ought to have them preg tested, he thought. *I'll see about that when I'm in town. I could probably get it done after I get the pasture fence built. I'll have to get another bull come spring, probably an Angus—they generally throw smaller calves, but they grow good.*

He didn't have much to do Thursday and Friday. On Saturday, he was up early and on his way to the sale barn. When he arrived, he went through the corrals and checked his calves and cows. They'd been fed well.

As he was looking over his cattle, the brand inspector approached. "These yours, Mud?"

"Yep. You need the papers filled out on 'em?"

"Yep. I can look at them here and fill out the papers. They look pretty good, don't they?"

"Yes. I hope the prices are good," replied Mud.

"Prices are up a little over last year, but not much."

"Anything helps!"

Mud signed the brand papers and went to the café to get a cup of coffee. He noticed a few familiar faces, but didn't talk to anybody. Most of his life he'd been a loner.

He took his coffee to the sale ring and got a front row seat. He thought he might bid a little on his own cattle just to push up the price, but he had to be careful—he didn't want to buy back his own cattle!

His cattle were after the fourth or fifth lot to be sold. They'd sorted the steers from the heifers and bunched them according to size. They ran the cull cows through and then his bull. He wrote down the prices they brought and did a little figuring. The bull didn't weigh as much as he thought he would, but he did have a little age on him. If his figures agreed with the figures when they made out the check, he thought he'd have a pretty good payday.

He watched the sale for another half hour or so, just long enough to give the office help time to make out the check. He picked up his check and studied it as he went to his truck. The commission house had deducted the trucking charges, which he thought were too much, but then he remembered he'd been told that the driver would probably want overtime. They'd also deducted feed and commission charges. Mud got to thinking that he was over charged and was about to go back and talk to the manager about it, but then decided against it. He didn't know what the price of hay was, and he had enough money to get all his supplies and have quite a bit left over.

He stopped at the bank to deposit his check, but it was closed. He'd have to mail his check to deposit it. Then it occurred to him that he didn't have any envelopes. He stopped at the drug store and bought a box of envelopes and a stamp. He only had one letter to mail and it upset him a little that he had to buy a box of envelopes, but he did it.

Before he went to the hardware store, he filled out his deposit slip, endorsed his check, put it in an envelope, stamped it, and went to the post office and mailed it. Confident that he had completed his monetary chores, he went to the hardware store to get his fencing supplies. He filled up with steel posts, barbed wire, and everything else on his list and had the clerk at the store help load it in his truck.

As he was paying for his supplies, he asked the clerk, "Do you know a welder that can make a steel post driver for me?"

"You don't need a welder," replied the clerk. "We have them available here. I'll show you where they are."

"They're probably more expensive than I want to spend," said Mud.

"With the prices welders are charging these days, they're not much more expensive. And you can take this one with you right now. You won't have to wait a couple of days until some welder gets around to it."

Mud was sold on the idea of taking it with him now. He didn't realize he'd have to wait a couple of days.

"This is a good heavy steel post driver," said the clerk, as he handed it to Mud.

"It seems plenty heavy," said Mud.

"That's the nice part," answered the clerk. "It's heavy enough that you can let it do the work. You just have to lift it."

"You mean," said Mud, "that this tool needs constant supervision?" Mud had decided to have some fun with the young clerk.

The clerk acted a little surprised and was taken aback a little. "Yes," he stammered out. "All our tools need to be used."

"You mean they need constant supervision!" replied Mud.

"I guess so," answered the clerk. "I don't think we have any tools that work alone."

"Then I ought to get a pretty big discount if I have to constantly supervise this piece of equipment," said Mud. "After all, my time's pretty valuable."

"I'm not really authorized to give any discounts," said the clerk.

"I probably ought to talk to the manager then," said Mud.

The clerk was becoming a bit frustrated and said, "I'll

call him." He reached for the store microphone and his voice stammered out over the store intercom, "Would Mister Peters please come to the front?" The word please was emphasized.

Presently, Mister Peters showed up and said, "Is this old reprobate giving you a problem, Walter?"

Walter looked surprised that Mister Peters would refer to a customer as an "old reprobate." But he didn't have an opportunity to answer. Mister Peters was already talking to Mud.

"Are you harassing my help, Mud?" said Mister Peters as he shook his hand. He was already acquainted with Mud.

"This young man says he's not authorized to give any discounts," said Mud. "Seeing as I'm going to have to constantly supervise this implement, I think I need some sort of a discount."

"That might be possible," said Mister Peters. "You've bought quite a bit here over the years, I think we could arrange something. Walter, put that post driver in his truck. I'll just give it to him."

Walter looked surprised, but did as he was told.

"How have you been, Mud? We haven't seen you around here for quite some time."

"I've been gettin' by all right. I've been up helping the Wilson's gather their cattle. I just barely escaped from their outfit."

"Escaped? I thought the Wilson's were pretty decent people," said Mister Peters.

"They are," replied Mud and deciding he'd said too much, he didn't say anything else. He paid his bill, thanked Mister Peters and drove back to his ranch. On the way, he got to thinking about his experience in town. He wondered if he had been nice enough to Mister Peters. He realized Peters was only trying to be neighborly. But, he'd always been uncomfortable in social situations. Actually he was a loner.

He also got to thinking that he ought to watch his words. Saying he'd "escaped" the Wilson's didn't sound too good, particularly for the Wilson's.

He got to his ranch and left the steel posts, wire, and all the fencing materials on the truck. He could unload them as he built fence. The sooner he got that done, the better he'd feel.

The next day, Mud was up early working on his fencing project. He secured a strand of barbed wire, about a foot off the ground, to his brace post and unrolled it from the truck as he drove toward the next brace. When he got to the brace, he cut the wire and tied it to the front bumper of the truck. Then he backed the truck up, tightening the wire. When he had it pretty tight, he set the brake on the truck and walked the length of the wire, freeing it from whatever brush it may have got hung up on. He walked back to the truck, freeing the wire where it had got hung up on more brush as he went. He wanted it as straight as possible.

When he got to the truck, he backed it up some more, taking the slack out of the wire and tightening it up. He could see the wire rising off the ground as he backed up and when the whole stretch of wire was about a foot off the ground, he set the brake on the truck and stapled the wire to the brace. He then cut the wire and wrapped the end around the post.

"I'll be a long time doin' this for five strands of wire," he said to himself. Living alone, he'd gotten in the habit of talking out loud to himself. "I better plant some steel posts before I string any more wire, it could be difficult trying to drive steel posts with barbed wire in the way. I'll put a steel post about every twenty-five feet or so."

He got back in the truck and drove about twenty-five feet down the new fence. "I guess I'll plant this post here," he said to himself as he got out of the truck, broke loose a bundle of steel posts, got the post hole driver and started driving the post into the ground. "I suppose it would be easier to plant each post as I take them off the truck. It'll be easier that way, and that post driver could get plenty heavy by the end of the day. That kid at the hardware store said it was a good one because it was heavy. He wasn't mistaken."

3

Breaking Horses

By the end of the week, he had his holding pasture completed. He'd even hung the gates. Before he was finished, he got to wishing that he'd done it earlier, like a few years earlier.

Other than hauling some feed to his cows and horses, he didn't have much to do during the winter. He thought he'd halter break the mustang colt Pat and Honey had left with him. "Or was it Honey and Sally that had left the mare and colt," he questioned himself. "My memory loss is becoming more frequent as I get older. Oh well, it don't make any difference. I might as well halter break the old mare, too. I'll probably just sell her as a broodmare. If I get her cleaned up a little, trim her mane and tail, she might look pretty good."

That night he got to thinking about the maverick bull that he, Pat, and Honey had tried to capture earlier in the year. They had him captured, but when they went to load him in the truck, he ran up the ramp and just kept going, right over the rack onto the hood of the truck, breaking the windshield and putting a good-sized dent in the hood. He laughed as he thought about this; he hadn't laughed when it happened because the bull had gored his saddle horse, which was standing in the corral with his intestines hanging out. He'd tried to save the horse, but after a few days he had to shoot it just to put it out of its misery.

They never did capture the bull, but Pat put an end to his maverick ways, permanently. He shot the bull and the three of them butchered him right on the spot. Because of this, Mud had more than a winter's supply of meat.

Pat had given him the spotted horse that had been gored and Mud used it most of the time. He had two other saddle horses, but they were starting to show their age a little. Of course with his artificial leg, he couldn't do a lot of rough riding, in fact he had to ride with his right leg extended out away from the horse. His knee didn't bend sideways.

The horse Pat had given him was a good one, plenty gentle and he could do just about anything asked of him. And he was quite a bit younger than his other two horses.

The next day he ran in the mustang mare and colt. He roped the mare and choked her down. When she fell to the ground and quit fighting, he slipped up the rope and put a halter on her with a long soft cotton lead rope on it. If she wore the halter with that lead rope, he could catch her anywhere in the corral.

"That's about as rough as we need to get with you, old girl," he said, as he took off his lariat rope and let the mare up. "Unless you make it rougher yourself," he added.

He coiled his rope, got back on the paint horse and roped the colt. He didn't have to choke down the colt—it only fought the rope a little. He slowly worked his way up the rope toward the colt. As he got closer, the colt fought a little harder and Mud just let him fight. As the colt tired, Mud kept getting closer and finally managed to pet him on the nose.

Instinctively the colt pulled back and Mud let him. When the colt stopped fighting, Mud petted him again. "I just need to show you that I'm not going to hurt you," said Mud. He'd been talking to the colt all the while he'd been working his way toward him.

Eventually Mud managed to get a halter on the colt and he tied him to the corral. "We'll just start teaching you about being tied now," he said. Then he got the end of the mare's lead rope, took a wrap around a corral post, and started working the mare toward the post. When he got the mare within two feet of the corral, he tied the mare up.

"I'll just let you two learn to be tied for the next little bit," he said, as he left. He figured about an hour would work for the first lesson in learning to be tied. He went to the house, got a drink of water, and returned to the corral to keep an eye on his students.

The horses were learning not to fight the rope. They would struggle, then give up and catch their breath. Then they'd struggle again. Pretty soon they'd learn that there was no getting away. After a while they'd get tired of slamming up against the fence and just stand still. That's what they were supposed to be learning.

When his first hour of teaching was done, he slowly worked his way up the lead rope of the colt and managed to pet him. "I ain't going to hurt you, youngster. You just have to learn that we're goin' to be friends."

He petted the colt as much as the young horse would let him, which wasn't much, and turned him loose. Then he worked his way up the rope to the mare. There wasn't much fight in the mare, she'd pretty well worn herself out. But he still had to be careful, he wasn't as agile with his artificial leg as he had been before and the mare didn't know he wasn't going to harm her. He managed to pet the mare some and turned her loose. He left the halters and lead ropes on both horses figuring it would be easier and gentler to catch them and repeat the lesson tomorrow. After a few days, both horses should have learned to yield to the rope.

Deciding he'd done enough for the day, he went to the house. He started to fix up a big pot of stew. The maverick bull that Pat, Honey, and he had killed was tough and he needed to fix the meat with plenty of moisture to tenderize it. As he was fixing his supper, it started to snow.

First snow storm of the year, he thought to himself. *It won't amount to much.*

4

Reflections

As he ate, Mud thought about his past. It had been some time since he'd seen Pat and Bud Wilson—better than twenty years. The last time he'd seen them, Sally was just a little girl. Before that, the three of them had spent a lot of time together, looking after Bud's father's cows and occasionally helping out the neighbors. Jimmy McIntyre's father had spent a lot of time with them. Then came the fight between Bud and him.

He couldn't remember what the fight was about, it was a long time ago. He remembered Pat was trying to break it up, but he'd got knocked out. When he came to, he was alone. He went to the bunkhouse, got his bedroll, saddled his horse, put a pack saddle on his spare horse, and rode off. He didn't look around for anybody to say goodbye, he just rode off. He didn't know where he was going, he just felt that he had to get away.

As he thought about it, it seemed like all his life he was running away from something. He wondered if he was a square peg in a round hole in this life. "That could be a possibility," he said to himself as he did the supper dishes. "Although I'm certainly more comfortable living like I'm living now."

As he reflected on the past, he remembered that when

he rode off, he just rode, not paying any particular attention to where he was going. He rode for about five days, just wandering around, when he stumbled upon an old deserted homestead. He made a camp at the homestead and decided he would make it his home for a while, although the cabin needed a lot of fixing up and the corrals were needing a lot of repair. There was an old wood-burning stove in the cabin that was serviceable, and the hand pump for the well worked even though the water had some rust in it. If he pumped enough, the rust should get cleaned out. There was a creek nearby and the water ran clear.

The corrals showed some signs of being used recently even though they needed repair. "Somebody probably kept some cows in here for a day or two," he said to himself as he surveyed the situation. "This just might make me a home for a day or two."

He had enough groceries to last for a week if he used them sparingly. "I'll just hole up here for a spell until I figure out what to do." He had no plans.

Mud had spent two days at the homestead when a lone rider showed up, who rode up to the cabin, got off his horse and walked into the cabin, just like he owned the place. Mud was fixing his noon meal and was surprised when the stranger walked into the cabin.

"Howdy," said Mud.

"What you doing here?" asked the stranger. His voice was gruff and not friendly.

"Just passing through," answered Mud. "Want something to eat?"

"Yeah," replied the stranger. "Who are you?

"I'm Dusty," answered Mud. "Who are you?"

"Harold," replied the stranger. "I'm ridin' for the Leanin' N. We use this cabin as a line shack occasionally." His voice was still gruff.

"The Leanin' N. I never heard of it," said Mud.

"It's a pretty big outfit. Its headquarters are about twenty-five miles south of here. I'm in charge of this section of the ranch."

"You the cow boss?" asked Mud.

"No," answered Harold. "I'm just in charge of this part of the ranch."

Just a fence rider, thought Mud, *trying to impress me with his own importance!*

Harold didn't seem too friendly and Mud decided to keep his thoughts to himself about Harold's position. "These beans will be ready right directly," said Mud. "You like beans?" Mud knew every cowboy was familiar with beans and whether or not they liked them, they managed to put up with them.

"They'll do," replied Harold, choosing to remain non-committal regarding the beans.

"Find a place to sit and eat," said Mud, as he put a big plate of beans on the table. "That old nail keg might make a chair." The furniture was lacking in the cabin.

Mud dished himself up a plate of beans and sat down at the table on the only chair in the cabin. Harold pulled the old nail keg closer to the table and started to eat.

They ate in silence and Mud studied Harold closely. Harold was about sixty, Mud guessed, average size with no outstanding features. From his mannerisms, Mud decided he wouldn't like to be paired up with him for long. Mud concluded that Harold had had a pretty rough past—the lines in his face were deep and his face was red. Mud couldn't tell if the redness in his face was from the sun or perhaps from too much liquor. A lot of cowboys drank too much, but generally only when they went to town.

When they finished, Harold got up from his nail keg and said, "You know I'll have to tell the boss you're camped here. He's supposed to bring me supplies day after tomorrow. How long you figurin' on staying?"

"Sure," said Mud. "Go ahead and tell him, I'm not hurtin' nothin'. I just thought I'd stay long enough to rest my horses. Bring the boss by when he shows up if you want."

Harold went outside to get his horse without even thanking Mud for the meal. He got on his horse and said, "I'll bring the boss by if he's so inclined. I'm not so sure he'll take kindly to you being here. He might run you off."

"Whatever," replied Mud. "Where's your camp?"

"My camp is about three hours to the east of here," answered Harold. Without even an invitation to drop by sometime, Harold rode off.

Not very neighborly, thought Mud.

5

Unexpected Happenings

Mud had spent a little time cleaning up the cabin but decided not to do anything else, thinking that if he was run off, it would be a waste of time. He was beginning to feel comfortable in his surroundings and might not want to leave if he got too comfortable. He spent the next day just puttering around. He did reset the shoes on his saddle horse and his packhorse. As he did this, he mumbled, "I'd better get into some town soon and get some new shoes for both horses. It won't be long before they're both barefoot."

The next day he was opening up a can of beef stew when a pickup truck pulled up to the cabin. Two men got out. Harold got out of the passenger side. Mud thought, *The man who had been driving must be the boss.*

He opened a second can of stew and added it to pot that was heating up on the stove.

He was surprised to hear a knock on the door. Harold had just walked in when he showed up previously. He went to the door, opened it and said, "Howdy gents. Come on in."

The two men entered and Mud said, "Hello Harold."

Harold didn't reply, he just nodded his head. He looked a little rougher than he did two days before, like he'd been on a two day drunk.

The other man didn't wait for Harold to introduce them, he said, "I'm Gene Fisher. I own the Leanin' N."

Mud shook the extended hand of Gene Fisher. "I'm Dusty," he said. He thought, *At least this guy is more cordial than Harold.*

"The Leanin' N doesn't fit the name Fisher," said Mud.

"Oh yes it does," replied Fisher. "We named it after my wife, Nancy. She says she's always leaning on me." He said that with a slight laugh and Mud immediately decided he liked him.

"Better sit and get somethin' to eat," said Dusty. "This stew is just about ready. Find somethin' to sit on."

Glancing around the room, Gene said, "I'll stand."

Harold took the nail keg and Mud said, "You can sit here."

"I'll stand," said Gene. "I've been sitting in that truck all morning. Standing will do me some good. I can stretch a little. It's been a pretty rough ride out here. That road is little more than a wagon path, just a couple of ruts in the sagebrush."

They ate in silence and when they were through, Gene asked Mud, "How long do you intend on staying here?"

"I just wanted to give my horses some rest," replied Mud.

"You can stay as long as you want," said Gene. "I don't think you're hurting anything."

"I don't intend to."

"Just make yourself to home. Looks like you've cleaned this place up a little. We don't have many cattle out this way and Harold here just keeps the fences up."

"I appreciate that," said Mud.

Gene and Harold made preparations to leave. Gene thanked Mud for the meal, something Mud noted that Harold hadn't done.

They left and Mud felt quite comfortable. "Might just as well do some more fixing up," he said to himself.

He spent the next couple of days fixing up the cabin and the corrals then he caught his horse and decided to explore the country. He'd never been in this area before and the country interested him. Harold had indicated that his camp was about three hours or so from his and he thought he'd ride in that direction.

The country was mostly sagebrush with a scattering of cedar and piñon trees. Higher up there were aspen and pine trees. He enjoyed his ride. It had been some time since he'd rode just to look at the country.

Presently, he found Harold's camp. It wasn't much different than his own camp, although Mud noted that his camp was in better shape since he'd made some repairs and cleaned it up a little. He decided that Harold wasn't a very good grounds keeper.

There were a couple of horses in the corral and it looked like they hadn't been fed for a day or two. There was a fair road leading up to the cabin.

He rode up to the cabin and while still on his horse, yelled, "Hello the house!" He didn't get a response and noted that there wasn't any smoke coming from the chimney. He yelled again and got no response.

He got off his horse and went to the door and knocked. Nobody answered. He entered the cabin and was surprised at what he found. The place was a mess, a total disaster. Dirty dishes filled the sink, papers were strewn all over the floor, clothes were scattered everywhere. There were some empty liquor bottles scattered on the floor.

In a corner he found Harold, lying on his bed. He walked over and shook him, but got no response. Harold felt strangely cold when he touched him. He was dead!

Mud was more than a little surprised. He hadn't expected to find a dead person as his neighbor. He left the cabin as he found it and went out and fed the horses. He decided that he should inform Gene Fisher of what he'd found. He didn't know where the Fisher Ranch was, other than it was south of his place about twenty-five miles. He was ready to head south to the Fisher Ranch when he thought, *It might be a good idea to go back to my place, get a good night's rest and take a packhorse and bedroll before I start out. I'm not even sure where I'm going.*

The next day he was up early, saddled his horse, put his bedroll on his packhorse, and started out to find the Fisher Ranch. It was slow going. He decided that if he headed southeast, he could find the road that led to Harold's cabin from the Fisher Ranch. After an hour and a half or so, he found a road and hoped it led to the main ranch.

Roughly four hours later, he rode into the Fisher Ranch. He had seen some cattle as he approached the ranch, but hadn't seen a person. As he rode past the barn, he saw some men working on some farm machinery. He rode up to them and asked, "Where's Gene Fisher?"

Without answering, they pointed to the main house.

Mud rode his horse over to the house. There wasn't a hitch rack in front of the house, so he hobbled his horses and approached the front door. He knocked on the door and was greeted by a pleasant looking woman.

"Can I help you?" she asked.

"I'm looking for Gene Fisher," replied Mud.

"I'm Missus Fisher," replied the woman. "Gene's in the office. Come in."

"I'm sorta dirty," replied Mud.

"What is it, Nancy?" asked Gene as he approached from the office. Seeing Mud, he said, "Hello Dusty, come in."

"I got some bad news for you Mister Fisher ..."

"Gene will do," interrupted Gene. "What's the news?"

"I rode over to Harold's camp just to explore the country and get better acquainted with him and found him dead," said Mud.

"Oh!" exclaimed Missus Fisher, visibly shaken.

"Nancy, you better sit down," said Gene. "Come in and tell me what happened, Dusty."

"Just like I said, I went in the cabin and found him dead. He'd been dead for a day or two, his horses were in the corral and hadn't been fed. I found him yesterday and thought I'd better let you know today. That's all I know, other than I fed his horses before I left."

Gene's attention was diverted momentarily by Nancy's crying. She was visibly shaken. Gene briefly tried to console her, then said to Mud, "Let's go out on the porch. We can figure out what to do out there."

"You'll have to excuse Nancy," said Gene, once they were outside. "Harold was her brother, my brother-in-law."

"I'm sorry," said Mud. "I didn't know."

"That's all right. He really wasn't much good. Drank too much. I just kept him around because he was family. He couldn't do much, so we kept him out in that line camp

28

where he couldn't get into any trouble. We better call the sheriff and have him come out with the coroner."

"I've done what I came here to do," said Mud. "I better be headed back, I've got a long way to go.

"You probably ought to stay here until the sheriff comes," said Gene.

"Why?" questioned Mud.

"The sheriff will want to talk to you, seeing as you're the one who found him. I see you've got a bedroll on your pack-horse, you can stay in the bunkhouse. The sheriff probably won't be here until later."

"I guess you're right," said Mud.

"Turn your horses loose in the corral, put your gear in the barn and take any unused bunk in the bunkhouse," said Gene. "I'll call the sheriff."

About an hour later the sheriff showed up with the coroner. After some preliminary questions, the sheriff said, "We better go examine the body. You come with us, Dusty."

They drove out to Harold's camp, the sheriff and coroner in the sheriff's car and Gene and Mud in Gene's truck. Everything was as Mud had left it the day before.

After an inspection of the cabin, the sheriff said, "There doesn't appear to be any foul play. We'll have the coroner do an autopsy to determine the exact cause of death and call this closed, if there's nothing extraordinary found during the autopsy. You might want to stay around close, Dusty."

"Why?" questioned Mud.

"You found Harold so that makes you a prime suspect if there was any foul play," replied the sheriff. "We won't know until the autopsy is completed."

Mud immediately became concerned. Could it be that he was accused of Harold's death? *That would be murder,* thought Mud.

"I'm sure everything is above board," said Gene. "Dusty will be at the ranch as long as necessary."

"I'll send an ambulance out tomorrow to bring in the body."

The coroner covered Harold's lifeless body with an old dirty blanket and they drove back to the Fisher Ranch.

The next day, an ambulance showed up and Gene and Mud accompanied it to Harold's camp. When the ambulance left, Gene fed Harold's horses and said, "I'll send a hand out with the ton and a half truck to get the horses tomorrow. As soon as the sheriff calls, you can go, Dusty. If he calls early in the day, you can load your horses in the truck and my hand can take you back to where you're camped. How long you gonna stay?"

"I don't know," replied Mud. "I'm kinda liking it up there, it's quiet and peaceable, although I don't like the idea of being a suspect in a case involving a death."

"Hum," said Gene. "Don't let the sheriff bother you. He's just doing his job. He's just a little overly cautious. We've never had any serious crime in this part of the country and the sheriff is just being thorough. I don't think you've got anything to worry about."

About noon the next day, the sheriff called and reported that there wasn't any foul play in the death of Harold. The coroner had listed his death as "acute alcohol poisoning." Mud was free to go, and he was really relieved. He'd had some real serious thoughts about being brought up on murder charges.

When Gene told Mud about the coroner's findings, he said, "Apparently Harold just drank himself to death. I knew it was coming, sooner or later. So did Nancy. I've been thinking, though, if you like staying where you are, why don't you come to work for me? I can pay you and provide you with groceries. You'll just have to keep an eye on what cattle are up there and do some fence fixing. Just what Harold was supposed to be doing. You'll pretty well be on your own."

"I'd need to think about that," replied Mud. "I don't really have any plans, don't know what I'm going to do."

"Think it over real quick," said Gene. "If you decide to take me up on my offer, I'll just have my hand leave Harold's two horses with you when he takes you up there. The horses are gentle enough. I can have a couple of hands haul the hay at Harold's over to you. If you use it sparingly, there should be enough to keep all the horses for the winter."

Without another thought, Mud took Gene up on his offer. The next day, Mud loaded his two horses in the truck, and along with one of Gene's hands, went to Harold's camp, loaded his two horses and then went on to his camp. Gene and Nancy followed in Gene's truck. Nancy wanted some of Harold's personal things, like his saddle, chaps, and hat.

After looking at Harold's cabin and the mess it was in, Nancy indicated to Gene that they should burn it. It really wasn't worth saving. Before Mud left for his camp, Gene told Mud, "Don't be concerned if you see some smoke coming from here, we've decided to burn the cabin and everything in it. I'll send some men out tomorrow to haul the hay over to you."

"It might be a good idea not to burn the cabin until the hay is hauled," suggested Mud.

"Good idea," said Gene. "I hadn't been thinking, what with all that's been going on here. You'll see the smoke in a few days, after all the hay is hauled. Thanks."

Mud just nodded and he and the hired man left for his camp. A few days later, he noticed smoke coming from the direction of Harold's cabin.

6

Back to Reality

Mud finished his reminiscing and went to sleep. When he awoke the next day, he was a little surprised to find about eight inches of snow on the ground. "It might be an early, long cold winter," he said to himself, as he went out to feed his mustang mare and colt.

It wasn't hard to catch the mustangs with the lead ropes dragging on the ground from the halters. It was a little harder to convince them that they should stand about an arm's length from the fence and not fight being tied up. Slowly but surely he managed to get the horses the proper distance from the fence and tie them up. Then he started petting them just like the day before, only today he brushed the snow off them. "A few more lessons like this and you'll be halter broke," he told them before he left.

It had turned a little cold and he went to the cabin to get another cup of coffee and warm up. He laughed at himself about the night before. He decided that he'd spent entirely too much time the night before reminiscing about the past. It had been some years since he'd given Harold and how he'd come to be here any thought. *Oh well,* he thought, *I guess it doesn't do any harm to reflect a little on the past.*

He noticed his horses coming in and thought about giving them a little hay, but then thought better of it.

"Once I start feeding them they'll quit looking for feed on their own and start expecting to be fed every day," he said to himself. "I'll run out of feed if I start feeding too early in the year. Maybe I ought to go give them a little grain, just to keep them close. If it storms more, they might drift with the storm and a little grain might help keep them around."

He went down to the corral where the horses had gathered, taking some grain from the barn as he went. He gave each horse a good-sized handful of grain. "Maybe I ought to try and give some to the mustangs. They don't know what it is, but they'll learn. Once they find they like it, it might make things a little easier."

The longer Mud lived alone, the more he talked to himself out loud. A lot of the time he was talking to the horses, but he found himself talking out loud even when he was in the house.

Mud went to the corral where the mustangs were tied. He got another measure of grain from the barn and slowly worked his way to the mare. She wasn't as fearful as she was yesterday, but she was still wary of the human. Mud let her smell the grain and she even put her head in the bucket to test it further. Mud didn't want to feed her from his hand, he might get bit. She got a mouthful of grain then suddenly pulled back, realizing she didn't trust the human. When she pulled back, she lost part of the grain she had.

"Maybe you got enough to think you like it," said Mud.

He then went to the colt and managed to give some to him. He spent more time with the colt and got him to take more grain. Then he went to the cabin to warm up and start a noon meal. He thought, *If it warms up tomorrow, I'll saddle a horse and ride out to see how my cows are doing. This storm hasn't brought them home.*

The next day he saddled a horse, the one Pat had given him was becoming his favorite, and rode out to look for his cows. He had to keep his right leg stretched out to the right, his artificial leg didn't curve around the horse. It was a little uncomfortable, but if he twisted himself in the saddle, kinda clockwise, he could manage. He found most of his cows and was a little surprised to find that one cow had calved.

"That maverick bull had been working overtime last year," he said. "I better take you two back to the ranch where I can keep an eye on you," he told the cow and calf. He slowly worked the pair toward the corrals.

"I suppose I can keep you in my new holding pasture," he said, as he closed the gate behind them. "I can keep a pretty close watch on you two here from the cabin. I suppose I'll have to start watching the cows a little closer. That won't be too difficult and it'll give me something more to do in the winter."

Mud didn't have much to do during the winter. He'd feed his horses and cows every day if there was a lot of snow on the ground, then walk down to the creek with an axe and chop a big hole in the ice so his livestock could drink. Other than that, he just had to take care of himself.

The storm broke the next day and Mud enjoyed about three weeks of warmer autumn-like weather—cool nights and warmer days. The snow melted and left the watering holes and creeks with plenty of water.

He'd made a lot of progress with the mustang colt and the colt was even coming up to meet him in the mornings when Mud started the training sessions. He was making slower progress with the mare. She had spent all her life out on the open range and progress with her was slower, but he was making some progress. She was ornery.

"Not a problem," he said. "I don't have anything but time and there's no rush. I am making progress and the mare don't know it, but I'm saving her life. If I didn't gentle her and halter break her, she might end up in a can of dog food or a tube of glue." Mud laughed as he thought about this.

He rode every day checking his cows, but didn't have any more calves hit the ground. He pondered over whether his first calf was an early calf or a late calf. He couldn't quite figure it out, but amused himself with the thought.

The weather turned cold again and although there wasn't any snow on the ground, it stayed cold. Mud knew that the snow, when it came, would stay on the ground all winter. He could wait for the snow.

When the snow did come, it came with a fury. One night alone, eighteen inches accumulated. And it continued during the day until more than two feet had fallen. And every day, more snow fell. This made feeding difficult. Mud had to use a packhorse to feed.

He'd pack a bale of hay on each side of the horse, they only weighed about seventy pounds apiece, then mount his own horse and lead the packhorse out to the cows and scatter the hay by hand. Eight trips like this took most of the day. He couldn't remember a winter like this since he'd landed at this old homestead. He decided he'd need to get a tractor to feed with. But he didn't know whether to get a tire tractor or a crawler. He'd figure that out when the time came. He didn't know how much a tractor cost, but he'd saved up a considerable amount of money over the years that he'd been on the place with a monthly check from the Fisher Ranch and selling off his own calves every fall. For the time being, he was stuck doing things as he was.

7

Remembering

The winter wore on and Mud caught himself wishing spring would come early. He was essentially snowed in.

One night, after he'd had his supper, he found himself looking over his bank book trying to figure out how much money he could spend on some sort of tractor. He was surprised at how much he had. Gene Fisher had deposited his paycheck directly into Mud's savings account every month. Mud hadn't paid any attention to the balance when Gene brought the deposit slip and bank statements to him. Mud knew how much was in his checking account because he'd add the checks from his calf sales into it and total it when he bought something in town. Most of the time the checkbook just stayed in the jockey box of the truck. He hadn't realized how much the Fishers had helped him out and he got to remembering how he'd come to run his own cows on that part of the Fisher Ranch.

It was a lot of years ago, but he remembered it as if it had happened yesterday. There were more Fisher cattle on that part of the range than Gene had thought. Mud managed to gather them all and Gene was surprised when he saw the numbers.

"I suppose Harold didn't do much for me out here," said Gene. "Probably just sat around and drank most of the time."

"Judging from what his cabin looked like, I suspect you're right," said Mud.

"I wonder where he got his booze from?" asked Gene.

"I bet someone brought it out to him," said Mud. "Not long after you buried him, I saw a truck headed down the road to his old cabin. I haven't seen it since."

"I wonder if they were surprised when they saw that the cabin had burned down?" asked Gene.

"Probably more disappointed than surprised," said Mud. "Somebody lost a good booze customer."

"Think so?"

"Sure," said Mud. "He had to be a good customer if his supplier would deliver way out here. I'll bet a lot of money traded hands out here."

"Maybe some cows too," added Gene. "Way out here, I wouldn't know and I'm sure Harold didn't even have an idea of how many cows he was supposed to be watching out for. You've gathered more cattle than I thought were here, Dusty ..."

"Just call me Mud," interrupted Mud. "Everybody else does."

"Dusty Waters. Mud? Makes sense. But as I was saying, Dusty ... ah, Mud, why don't you run a few cows out here?"

"I wouldn't think of asking to use your range and feed to run my own cows," said Mud.

"Well, now wait a minute," said Gene. "I'm suggesting the idea, and if you had a few cows of your own, I wouldn't have to worry about you selling some of mine for me and not telling me. After all, Harold was my brother-in-law and I wouldn't be surprised if he sold a few of my cows and pocketed the money for himself. You're almost a stranger." Gene had a grin on his face when he said that.

Mud didn't know if Gene was joking or not, but took offense. "Gene, if you think I'd steal one of your cows, you got another thing coming! I have about everything I need here and I certainly don't need to steal anything from anybody!"

"Don't get upset, Dusty ... ah, Mud," said Gene. "I just said that to see what your reaction would be. And I thought it was kinda funny. But I still think it would be a good idea to have a few cows of your own. This range will handle more cattle than I thought—you proved that by how many cows you've gathered. And they're all in good shape."

"I don't know," said Mud.

"Besides, it might be a good way to keep a good man on the payroll," said Gene.

"If you insist," said Mud. "But don't you think I'll spend more time looking after my cattle than yours?"

"Nope. They'll all be running together," answered Gene. "I'll get you started with a few older cull cows and you can add to them as you wish. I'll get you the cows after we've weaned their calves. They should all be pregnant."

"Okay," said Mud.

That fall, a stock truck showed up at Mud's cabin with six cows in it. Gene was driving the truck. "This is your herd, Mud," he said.

"Six cows don't hardly make a cow herd," said Mud. "But I appreciate it. I'll need to get 'em branded but I don't even have a brand registered."

"You can take care of that later. Each one has a black stripe painted on her left side to mark her as yours. The paint should last all winter and come spring, you can buy or build a chute, register a brand, and brand them. You're in the cow business!"

Inside, Mud felt quite proud. But he didn't want it to show. He calmly thanked Gene and turned the cows into the corral. As he looked them over, he decided they might last another year or two. They all had some age on them. By then he should have some replacements picked out.

Gene said, "I'll send some men out with some loads of hay. We'll send enough to get the cattle and horses through the winter. I'll have to bill you for the hay your cows eat but I'll take it out of your wages. You probably won't miss it."

"That's fine," replied Mud.

Gene left and Mud went to the house for the evening.

The next day Mud was up early, feeding. Loading the packhorse with a bale of hay on each side was difficult. He'd load a bale on one side then have to hurry and load another bale on the other side. If he took too long, his packhorse would become uncomfortable with the unbalanced load and buck it off. The horse didn't give him any leeway because of his artificial leg. He would place a bale on one side of the horse, then, as fast as he could, he'd load another one on the opposite side. More than once he had to reload a bale.

Mud spent the winter feeding his livestock and himself. He spent a little time, generally after supper, reminiscing about his past and sometimes, when he finished, he felt a little guilty and wished he'd done things differently. He didn't dwell on his guilt too much, "What's done is done," he'd say to himself.

He had particularly fond thoughts about how he got electricity into the house. After an unusually cold winter,

Gene drove into the yard one day and honked the horn. Mud came to the door dressed in just about everything he had. Even though it was early spring, it was still cold, just as cold as it had been during January.

Mud waved for Gene to come into the house and Gene came inside. He was surprised that there was ice on the inside of the windows.

"You need better heat in here," said Gene. "Let's go talk in the truck, it's warmer in there."

"It's only cold in the morning," replied Mud, "until I get a fire going."

They went to the truck. "It is warmer in here," said Mud.

"Well, I'll bet it got plenty cold last winter."

"It did," said Mud. "It provided a real incentive to get up and build a fire. But gettin' this place to warm up a little caused me to be a little late feeding everything, but they got fed every day."

"I think we'll see about stringing electricity out here. Then you'll have some heat. I'd hate to come out here and find that you've froze to death."

"That would be kinda nice, but wouldn't it be expensive?"

"You let the Fisher Ranch worry about that," said Gene. "You've done a good job out here and a little extra reward is warranted."

Later in the spring, when the ground had thawed, the electric company set poles in the ground, strung wire and Mud had electricity in the house. Mud decided to keep the oil heater, as he liked the heat from it better than the electric heat.

Some years later, occasionally during the winter, he'd spot a new calf that had been born during the night. He'd be surprised that they'd been able to survive the cold, and was grateful that they had. He had the wild bull that Pat had shot to thank for the early calves. "Won't be a very uniform calf crop," he said to himself, as he brought a calf and its mother closer to the ranch house. "I guess this spring I'll have to go buy a bull."

Since he'd been up to help the Wilson's gather cattle, his thoughts had been more and more of Bud, Pat, and their early days together. The three of them had been almost inseparable from their teenage years. "Funny," he said, "Bud's in a wheelchair and I'm crippled with an artificial leg. The only one still getting around anywhere like normal is Pat. And Pat always got the worst end of everything that happened. Like the wild horse race at the fair and rodeo one year."

Mud smiled as he thought about that. Bud was the roper, Pat was the mugger, and Mud was the rider. Bud didn't have any problem roping the wild horse, but Pat had his hands full trying to hold the horse so Mud could get the saddle on and then get on the critter. Bud was choking the horse down, Pat was trying to hold his head and Mud was trying to get the saddle on. Pat did get a halter on the horse.

Mud laughed out loud as he remembered Pat hollering, "Hurry up Mud! This critter is pounding me to death!"

The horse was striking at Pat with his front feet and making contact. The horse would rear up, lifting Pat off the ground a good seven or eight inches. Pat managed to hold on, but was having a rough time of it. The horse was being choked down, but still had a lot of fight in him.

Mud managed to get the saddle on the horse and cinched

it down tight before the horse fell. The horse's head landed on Pat, knocking the wind out of him. He lost his grip on the horse and lay prostate on the ground.

Mud got on the horse while it was on the ground. Bud gave the horse some slack and it got up. Mud almost fell off when the horse got up, but managed to get straight in the saddle. When the horse got up, it stepped on Pat's leg.

Bud acted as a hazer, trying to drive the wild horse toward the finish line. He had to drop his rope as another team's wild horse ran between Bud and the wild horse. Mud was holding on for dear life and not trying to guide the horse. He was depending on Bud to run the horse toward the finish line. They crossed the finish line, but not first. There were two other teams that finished before them, so they ended up third.

Mud's horse kept running and Bud hollered to Mud, "Just stay on him! I'll get you!"

Bud caught up to the wild horse, got the lead rope, dallied up and took Mud off. "Just like plucking an apple off an apple tree," he said as he set Mud on the ground. "Get your saddle and we'll turn this critter loose."

Mud loosened the cinch and let the saddle fall to the ground. He took off the halter and Bud's lariat rope.

"We better see how Pat is," said Bud, looking around toward Pat. He was still lying on the ground, motionless. "He might be hurt pretty bad, he hasn't moved."

They went over to where Pat was. The medical people had gathered around him.

"How is he?" asked Bud.

"I think he just had the wind knocked out of him," said

one of the medics. "He'll probably be all right, but we need to take him to the hospital to check for any broken bones."

"I'm okay," muttered Pat as he sat up with the help of the medics. "I sure don't need to go to the hospital!"

Pat struggled to his feet. "How'd we do?" he asked.

"We came in third," answered Mud. "We'd have done better if you could have held the horse. I had a tough time gettin' the saddle on."

"*You* had a tough time! You should have been where I was!" exclaimed Pat.

"You sure you're all right?" asked Bud.

"Yep," replied Pat. "Just some bruised ribs, I think."

"You need to let us take you to the hospital," said the medic.

"Nope," replied Pat. "It would cost us what little money we made."

Mud laughed as he remembered the wild horse race. "Those were the good old days," he said to himself.

8

Bad News

Mud spent the rest of the winter feeding his cows and staying warm. More than once, as he loaded hay in the truck to feed, he thought about having to load hay on a packhorse to take to the cattle. He laughed at himself, and his crude earlier methods, but was satisfied he had gotten the job done. He'd built himself up a fairly nice herd of cattle. He wasn't happy that the renegade bull had been providing him with calves almost year round, but they had remedied that.

As spring approached, he found himself making preparations for his garden. It was located on the other side of the hill from the house, close to the creek. He'd dug a ditch so he could irrigate his crops. He'd also built a six-foot high fence around the garden plot to keep the deer and elk out. He'd bought his seed last fall, so he could start planting the garden as soon as the ground thawed out.

It was a short walk over the hill to his garden spot, but it took longer with his artificial leg. One day he walked to the garden spot to check the ground and found it thawed enough to start working the soil before he started planting. He went back to the house, got a shovel and a hoe and returned to the garden.

As he started working the dirt, he had to laugh at himself as he remembered the first year he had planted a garden—

he'd hoed out a whole row of young corn plants thinking they were weeds. *I'll have to be more careful,* he thought to himself. He was more careful every year since.

Mud didn't really fancy himself a gardener, but he did enjoy having a garden. He often wondered what his old cowboy friends would think if they saw him tending a garden. He thought they would mock him—the rough, tough, fearless, ride anything cowboy—if they knew how much he enjoyed the garden, even the irrigating.

He didn't spend all his time in the garden. He'd turned his cows out and he rode through them two or three times a week. The young mustang colt had been halter broke and had gentled down nicely. He'd gentled down the colt's mother and was riding her around in the corral. He hadn't taken her outside the corral, but that was coming. She turned nicely and was learning how to stop. Mud thought he'd take her outside the corral when she became a little more trustworthy.

One day, when the snow was gone, except for the high mountain peaks and shady areas on the north aspect of the steeper hills, Mud went to town for gas and propane. He'd been alone all winter and hadn't seen a soul. He wasn't hungering for company, but the sight of another human being didn't seem all that distasteful.

He went to a restaurant, got some cooking that wasn't his own, filled his propane and gas tanks, and went to the post office to check his mail.

His mailbox was filled with flyers and outdated advertisements. There was one letter, which surprised him. He wasn't used to getting letters and wondered who it was from and what it could be. The return address read the Wilson

Ranch, and he was immediately curious. He was reading it as he crossed the parking lot of the post office and almost got hit by a car backing out of a parking space.

"Sorry," said the driver of the car, "I didn't see you."

"That's obvious," replied Mud, in a somewhat irritated tone.

"You want to make something of it?" replied the driver in an equally irritated tone, ready to get out of the car.

"Nope," replied Mud. "You're all right. Just got some bad news, that's all."

"Sorry," said the driver again and he drove off.

Jerk, thought Mud. *Why don't he watch where he's going?* It didn't occur to Mud that he was reading the letter and not watching where *he* was going.

The letter read:

Hello old friend Mud,

    Hope this finds that you have wintered well. Things are fine at the Wilson Ranch and look to continue that way. Bud wanted me to warn you, LOOK OUT!
Best,
Pat

"Not much of a letter," mumbled Mud. "But at least it's a letter and a warning at that. I wonder what the warning is about. That's just like Pat. Send me a warning and not tell me what to watch out for!"

Mud pondered the situation, couldn't figure out why he should be warned, pocketed the letter and drove home. He didn't give the warning any thought, confident that he could handle himself in any situation.

He got back to his ranch, unloaded the gas tanks and cans, fixed some supper and went to bed.

The next day, he did some gardening then saddled the mustang mare. He figured on riding her around in the small holding pasture he'd built the fall before. That way, if she bucked him off, at least she couldn't get away. The mare was standing well for him to get on. Getting on was difficult with his artificial leg.

He rode the mare around in the corral, then opened the gate and went into the holding pasture. The mare didn't try to run off when they were out in the pasture and Mud thought she might enjoy being rode someplace other than in the corral. They were having a nice leisurely walk around the pasture when a sage hen flew up almost underneath them. The mare had spooked the sage hen. The mare wasn't used to such strange things happening and she started bucking.

Mud had figured himself to be a pretty fair bronc rider in his younger days, before he acquired an artificial leg, but the mare was getting the best of him. It wasn't long before he hit the ground. His main concern was that the artificial leg would get caught up in the stirrup and he'd be dragged—possibly to death. He was relieved that the artificial leg cleared the stirrup, although he hit the ground hard and it pained him.

He'd had the mecate on his hackamore tucked into his belt and instinctively reached for it while he was in the air, before he hit the ground, so he had the mare, even though he was on the ground. He lay on the ground for a minute trying to figure out if he was hurt badly. The mare was standing a few feet away, watching him. He swore that the mare had a look on her face that seemed to ask, "Did I do that?"

He had some pain in his right hip and thought it might be broken. He tried to move and found that he could, but with considerable pain. He thought, *That's a fine howdy do! If I need a hip replacement, it won't be long before I'm made up of spare parts. Leftovers from some old car or washing machine or something.*

He struggled to his feet and took a few tentative steps toward the mare. She hadn't seen him get up before and thinking that this was some strange creature designed to hurt her, she backed up and tried to get away. Mud kept a hold on the mecate and the mare couldn't get away.

Talking soothingly to the mare, Mud approached her. Hearing the sound of his voice, the mare calmed down. "Now, old girl, if you'll stand so I can get on, I'll ride you home. I don't want you thinking if you buck me off, you don't have to carry me back! That could be a very bad habit for you to develop!"

With some difficulty, Mud got on the mare. His hip hurt, but he thought it wouldn't be as bad riding as walking back to the corrals. The mare stepped out, gingerly, not knowing what to expect. Feeling the tenseness within the mare as she stepped out, Mud said, "I guess that sage hen did scare you, old gal. Well, don't worry about it, she scared me too!"

Having gotten in the saddle, Mud decided he should ride around a little longer. He wanted to end his ride on a positive note, without the memory of the bucking incident fresh in the mare's mind. He rode around for another half hour or so then turned toward the corrals.

The pain in his hip wasn't as bad and Mud decided it

wasn't broke. At the corrals, he got off the mare, somewhat painfully, unsaddled her, grained her, patted her on the neck and turned her loose. He decided that he'd have to sack her out some more—get her more used to things flopping around her. He'd start on that tomorrow. Right now he needed to get a little rest and do something to relieve the pain in his hip.

He went to the barn, got an old bottle of horse liniment, went to the house, stripped down and applied the liniment liberally to his hip. He lay down on the bed and tried to relax, letting the liniment work. As he lay there, he thought about the incident.

"No, the mare didn't buck all that hard, but she did throw me," he said to himself. "I guess I'm not the bronc rider I thought I was. Either that, or I'm getting older. Of course this artificial leg doesn't help."

Lying on the bunk, he got to thinking about the wreck that brought about the artificial leg. It didn't seem all that serious at the time. A particularly tough horse he was riding had spooked in the trees and started bucking. He didn't know what spooked the horse, probably a deer or elk that jumped up suddenly. Mud was doing a good job of riding until the horse slammed him into a tree. His right knee took a pretty good hit against the tree and all of the sudden he didn't have any strength in his right leg. A couple of jumps later and the horse had bucked Mud off. He landed on his right knee, then the horse stepped on it. He felt the pain immediately. He couldn't bend his right knee. He managed to get back on the horse and ride him home.

That night his knee had swelled up to the size of a football and he had a hard time getting around. He thought he ought to go to the doctor, but he was in a cow camp a long way way from town. He decided he could manage. Thus the start of years of a painful knee that just got worse as time went on. Finally, he did go to the doctor and after a considerable amount of time trying to fix the knee without success, he had a knee replacement, which unfortunately kept getting infected.

After a year or so of having the doctor tend to the knee infection with no noticeable improvement, and numerous trips to town, the doctor told him, "We're not making any improvement with this knee infection and it doesn't look like we will. We can continue to try and improve it, but the outcome isn't very promising. Or we can amputate it. The decision is yours."

Mud remembered asking, "How long will it take?"

The doctor replied, "The surgery won't take too long in itself. But it will take some time to heal, then some physical therapy teaching you how to use an artificial leg. All in all, I'd say a couple of months."

Mud thought about it, then said, "Let's do it in the winter. There's not as much riding and I can take the time then."

"Are you sure?" asked the doctor. "This is a very serious move and it will impact you and your actions for the rest of your life. Of course, the infection that we can't seem to clear up could kill you."

"Let's do it. My actions have been impacted for the last few years by this knee and the pain has been almost unbearable. I'd be better off without it, or the pain. Let's do it in December."

"Okay," said the doctor. "But you'll need to sign a release as this is a completely voluntary operation. You won't be able to hold the hospital or me responsible for the outcome."

"Fine," answered Mud. "I don't hold anybody responsible for anything, except myself."

"If that's what you want," said the doctor. "You'll have a few months to reconsider before we do the amputation, but it's our best recourse at this point."

"I don't need any time to reconsider," said Mud. "My minds made up. We'll do it!"

They set a date for the operation and Mud didn't give it a second thought.

Mud made arrangements with Gene Fisher to have one of his hands come out and do the feeding for a few months while Mud was having the operation and physical therapy. Gene tried to talk Mud out of the operation but without success. Gene ended his argument with the statement, "You know you'll be handicapped for the rest of your life!"

"Yep," replied Mud. "But I'll be better off and pain free!"

9

Hospital Life

December came and the hand from the Fisher Ranch showed up. Mud spent a day or two showing him what needed to be done. Before he left, Mud's final instruction was, "Keep the house clean!"

The Fisher hand gave Mud a funny look. Apparently he didn't think the house was too clean to start with. Mud drove to town and checked in at the hospital. The nurse gave him a funny look when he told her he was Dusty Waters.

"But Mister Waters," said the nurse, "your operation isn't until tomorrow."

"Well, I'm here today," said Mud.

"But Mister Waters, your operation is scheduled for four o'clock tomorrow afternoon!" The nurse was becoming more stern.

"I'd rather be early than late," replied Mud.

"You need to be here around noon tomorrow to make preparations."

"Well, I'm here now and ready."

"We won't have a room for you until tomorrow," said the nurse. "You come back around noon tomorrow and we'll be ready for you."

"What do I do until noon tomorrow?"

"You'll need to get a hotel room."

Mud left to get a hotel room. He had a strange feeling that he wasn't going to enjoy his hospital stay. After checking into the hotel, he went to get something to eat. He'd heard about hospital food and decided he'd better fill up.

He spent a restful night and showed up at the hospital a little before noon. The same nurse was on duty that was there the day before.

"I see you returned," said the nurse.

"Were you hoping I wouldn't?" asked Mud.

"Oh, certainly not," replied the nurse. "Your room is ready. If you'll just sit in this wheelchair, a nurse will take you to your room."

"I don't need a wheelchair!" retorted Mud.

"Hospital regulations," replied the nurse. Before Mud could say anything, the nurse added, "It's either the wheelchair or no room!"

Reluctantly, Mud sat in the wheelchair. As he was being wheeled to his room, he thought he ought to be wheeling the old lady that was wheeling him. She looked old enough to be his mother. But he decided not to say anything.

When they got to the room, the nurse handed him a hospital gown and said, "Take off your clothes. Put this on and get into bed."

Mud looked the gown over. "This nightshirt doesn't have a back! And it's too early to go to bed!"

The old nurse said, in a very stern manner, "Just do as you're told, cowboy. You'll get along better here if you do that."

The old nurse apparently had previous experience dealing with difficult patients. Mud wasn't trying to be difficult, it was just his way. He wasn't used to dealing with strangers, or anyone for the matter.

Mud did as he was told and got into bed, even though it wasn't even the middle of the afternoon yet. He felt uncomfortable. It wasn't long before the doctor showed up and tried to talk him out of the operation.

Mud wouldn't stand for it. As soon as he figured out what the doctor was trying to do, he said, "It's no use Doc. I've made up my mind. It's coming off! I've suffered long enough, too long actually!"

The doctor had him fill out the release forms and said, "The anesthesiologist will be in before four o'clock and start to put you under and ..."

"Not six feet under, I hope," interrupted Mud.

"You'll have to talk to him about that," said the doctor, with a grin on his face.

Around three-thirty, the anesthesiologist came in. "I'm here to put you to sleep," he said.

"I'm not worried about going to sleep," said Mud. "It's the waking up I'm concerned with!"

"Oh, there's an extra charge for that!" said the anesthesiologist, smiling.

As Mud drifted off to sleep, he was thinking, *It's strange how these people who worked so close to death all the time try to have a sense of humor.*

The next day, before sunrise, Mud woke up. It took him a minute or two to realize where he was. There was a nurse present.

"Did they get it off?" he asked. "That was the best I've slept in years!"

"Yes. The doctor tells me the operation was a success," replied the nurse. "They did tell me that you didn't want to wake up."

"That was a good sleep. I wish I could sleep like that every night!"

Mud couldn't feel his lower right leg. There was some pain, but not as much as there had been. Mud was still groggy and tried to sit up, but without success.

"Just lay there and rest," said the nurse. "You've been through a lot. The effects of the anesthesia will wear off shortly."

Mud did as he was told. He couldn't do much more. He looked around the room and noticed a set of crutches in one corner, but out of reach.

The nurse noticed, smiled and said, "You're not quite ready to be moving around yet. You'll start physical therapy tomorrow."

Mud lay back down, resigned to his fate. He became awfully bored in the hospital room.

The nurse left the room but returned fifteen minutes later. "I brought you some reading material," she said, as she put a bundle of magazines on the nightstand.

"Not women's magazines, I hope," said Mud.

"Certainly not!" the nurse said.

Mud was surprised to see that they were horse and cattle magazines. He started to read one when another nurse entered the room carrying a tray.

"Put that away," she said. "It's time to eat breakfast."

"I'm not really much of a breakfast eater," said Mud. "Just some coffee will do."

"You'll eat this if you know what's good for you," replied the nurse. "We've never had a patient starve to death at this hospital!"

Mud decided he'd better do what he was told. He thought, *This is a pretty tough bunch of old nurses here.*

During the afternoon, the final effects of the anesthesia had worn off and Mud began to feel more normal. He sat up in bed, got out and hopped over to where the crutches were in the corner. As he moved around, a nurse entered the room.

"What are you doing out of bed?" she exclaimed.

"I need to use the bathroom," answered Mud.

"There's a bedpan for that," replied the nurse.

"I've never used one of 'em before," said Mud. "You'd best get out of the way or we'll both be sorry!"

Flustered, the nurse moved aside and watched Mud go, who was smiling broadly.

"Where's the men's room?"

"Down the hall to the left," replied the nurse.

Unaware that his backside was showing, Mud hobbled down the hall to the men's room. He became aware of his state of partial undress while there. Upon finishing his business, he went to the door, opened it and looked both ways before leaving. The coast was clear and he hurried back to his room as fast as he could, unaccustomed to the crutches. He made it back to the room where the nurse was waiting for him.

"Where'd you put my clothes?"

"They're hanging up in the closet," answered the nurse.

"Well, let's put 'em close to the bed where I can get 'em when I need 'em."

"You won't be needing them until tomorrow," said the nurse. "They'll be just fine where they are."

The next day, Mud was up early as was his custom. He'd managed to get his pants on when a male nurse showed up.

"I'm your physical therapist. My name is Mike. Have you used crutches before?"

"I'm sorta familiar with 'em," replied Mud.

"Let's see how you get along with them. Walk across the room."

"I know how to use 'em," said Mud, irritated at the childish way he thought he was being treated. But he followed Mike's instructions.

Mike watched and said, "It's nice to know that you already know how to use them. We won't have to spend a lot of time on that. My real purpose is to teach you how to use your artificial leg."

"When do I get it?"

"It's being built as we speak. However, we need to let the leg heal properly before we try to fit it. The swelling must go down and the stitches need to be removed. We can't rush Mother Nature. We're working on her time schedule. It just takes time."

"What do I do in the meantime?" asked Mud.

"You can just relax. Or you can visit with the other patients in the lounge or cafeteria. Maybe watch some TV in the lounge. I don't see you having any difficulty with the crutches.

"Sounds like a meantime to me," said Mud.

Mike laughed and left the room.

Mud put on his shirt and his boot on the foot he still had. He got the crutches and started out of the room. The

59

empty pant leg bothered him as he hobbled down the hall. He stopped a nurse in the hall and asked, "Can I get a pin or something to hold this empty pant leg up? I don't want to trip myself!"

The nurse got a safety pin and pinned the pant leg up. Mud thanked her and asked her, "Where's the lounge?"

The nurse studied Mud carefully. He was unshaven and his clothes were wrinkled. Figuring him for a drunk, she replied, "We don't have a bar in this hospital."

"I don't need a drink," replied Mud, irritated at the nurse's assumption. "Mike told me there was a lounge where I could watch some TV. I don't have one out on my ranch."

"That's down this hall to the elevator on the left and down on the first floor."

"What floor are we on?" Mud felt funny asking the nurse that question. It made him feel like he didn't know where he was. Of course he didn't know where he was, they'd brought him up here while he was still under the anesthetic.

"We're on the third floor," replied the nurse.

Mud turned to leave. As he went down the hall, the nurse gave him a look that seemed to say, "Poor soul!"

After a few days of watching television and deciding there wasn't anything on worth watching, Mud spent more time in his room. The doctor checked on him daily. During one such visit, the doctor said, "This is healing nicely. I think we can get your artificial leg fitted and commence teaching you how to use it in another day or two."

"Fine," said Mud. "This place is driving me nuts! There's nothing to do. The sooner the better."

"Good. We'll start tomorrow. I'll have Mike come up and take you to physical therapy," said the doctor.

The next day, before Mike came to start physical ther-apy, Mud had a visitor. Gene Fisher came to see him. Mud was surprised.

"How's things on the Fisher Ranch?"

"They're good," replied Gene. "And they're good over on the Water's spread."

"The Water's spread? What do you mean by that?"

"Yep," replied Gene. "I went by on my way over here. My hired man says everything is okay. He's ridden your horses, checked your cows and mine and even wants to settle down there. He likes the place."

"I guess that's good," replied Mud. "What's this about the Water's spread?"

"Nancy and I have been talking. As you know, we don't have any kids or close relatives to pass our place onto when we die. So, we thought we'd deed this section to you so as you'd own it when we pass."

"Don't talk like that," said Mud. "You've got a lot of time left. Both of you will outlive me!"

"That's probably right," said Gene. "But with you becom-ing a one-legged man, you won't be able to move around as freely as you might like. It's time you put down some roots and stayed in one place."

Mud didn't know what to say. He took a little offense at being referred to as "a one-legged man" but it was true.

"Course, we'd still want you to watch our cattle on that part of the ranch, and we'd still pay you a wage for doing it."

"I don't know what to say," said Mud.

"You don't have to say anything," said Gene. "It's al-ready done. I've filed the papers with the courthouse al-ready. You'll get your papers in the mail within a couple of weeks. I've also deeded all the water rights to you. You'll be self-sufficient."

"What do I owe you for this?" asked Mud.

"Nothing, other than I'll take the filing fees out of your wages," replied Gene.

"Wages? I shouldn't have much coming after this stay in the hospital."

"Your wages have continued during your absence. You haven't had a vacation since you started. But you've had one now, although it might not have been as nice as a regular vacation. Course, you've had a nice rest."

"Rest!" exclaimed Mud. "I've been bored to death since I've been here. I can't wait to leave. I haven't done anything for days!"

"When can you leave?" asked Gene.

"Whenever Mike, the physical therapist, says so," answered Mud. "I've been trying to convince him I'm good to go now, but he's not convinced I can handle this artificial leg good enough to be let out on my own."

"All in due time," said Gene. "Just take your time. My hired man can stay at your place as long as you're here."

"I appreciate that," said Mud.

Mud's stay at the hospital was finally over and he returned to his place, but not after he got some extra groceries in town. Driving the truck was awkward with his new leg, but he just took it easy and drove slow. The only problem he had was braking. He'd spent too much time in the hospital doing nothing and was anxious to get back to work. When he got to his place, he unloaded his groceries with the help of Gene's hired hand, thanked him and sent him back to the Fisher Ranch.

The hired man didn't want to go. "Don't you need some extra help until you get used to your routine?" he asked.

"Nope," replied Mud. "I'll get used to it soon enough. I'll have to do it by myself anyways!"

The hired man left and Mud saddled a horse and with some difficulty, got on. It felt good to be in the saddle again, although he had to sit in the saddle a little different. He wouldn't really be able to give the horse adequate leg cues with his right leg. He'd have to get used to that and try to cue the horse with a shift in his weight in the saddle.

He rode out, found most of his cattle and determined that Gene's hired man had done a good job. He was satisfied. His horses were also in good shape.

10

The Big Blow

The morning after the mustang mare had bucked him off, Mud woke up and found himself in considerable pain. His hip hurt and he found it difficult to get out of bed. Not content to just lie there, he strapped on his artificial leg and struggled to get up. In pain, he struggled to the corner of the room where he stored his crutches and got them. *This will be less painful,* he thought as he hobbled outside to do his chores.

It was difficult to do his chores on crutches, but being able to support himself on the crutches took the pressure off his hip and he managed to get his chores done. *It'll be rough to continue this way,* he thought, *I hope my hip gets better quick.*

He hobbled back to the house and fixed himself a cup of coffee. As he sat in the house drinking it, he said to himself, "I'd better confine myself to the easier stuff until my hip gets better. Let's see now, just what can I do?"

As he thought about it, he decided he couldn't do much. He thought about all he could do was some gardening. Spring has arrived, so he should be able to start, although he didn't look forward to doing everything on crutches. He fixed himself another cup of coffee and pondered how he would get himself to his garden patch with a shovel and a hoe. He finally decided he would tie the shovel and hoe to each one of the crutches with baling twine and drag them to the garden.

It was awkward walking to the garden on crutches and dragging the tools, but he slowly made it. He thought about his predicament as he hobbled to the garden. Strangely, he didn't hold any resentment toward the mustang mare that had bucked him off the previous day. He reasoned that the mare had reacted naturally to the sage hen flying up beneath her. But he did look forward to having a sage hen supper at some point in the future.

He got to the garden spot and decided all he could do was clean the ditch. He started, although the crutches limited the amount of work he could do. He tried to work without the crutches, but it was too painful to his injured hip to support his weight. He struggled and his progress was slow. He spent most of the day cleaning ditch, and because his movements were slow, he decided to quit early. It would take him some time to get back to the house and do his chores.

He got back to the house, did his chores, and decided to spend some time with the mustang mare and colt. They were both gentle and came to him when he approached. "I'm sorry kids," he said as he petted them. "I didn't go to the barn to get a handful of grain for you. It's difficult to walk on these crutches. If you hadn't bucked me off yesterday, old gal, I would have gotten you a treat."

With his chores done, Mud went to the house to fix himself some supper. "Hopefully," he said to himself, "this hip will feel better tomorrow."

The next day, Mud's hip wasn't any better. "This is liable

to take some time," he muttered. "I'll just do what I can and go from there."

After a few days, Mud's hip finally started to feel better. He got to the point where he could walk without the crutches. When he felt he could handle it, he saddled the horse Pat had given him and rode out to check his cows. It was good to be in the saddle again. Finding his cattle to be in good shape, and a few calves on the ground, he started back to the house. He decided he should go along the creek and check his water supply. He didn't clean the ditch all the way to the creek when he was cleaning ditch, it was too far. He needed the water to irrigate his garden during the summer.

He got to the creek and much to his surprise, found it dry. "Something strange is going on here," he told his horse. "I wonder if someone is messing with my water supply. We'll have to ride farther up and find out what's happening."

Mud rode up the dry creek trying to figure out what was going on. As far as he knew, he owned all the water rights to the creek, and if someone had diverted his water, they were breaking the law. As he thought about it, he became more upset, reaching the point of becoming mad. "I'll get them water thieves," he said out loud.

About a mile and a half up the dry creek, he found where the water had been diverted. He laughed at himself and his anger. It wasn't people that had diverted the water, it was beavers. They had built a dam on the creek, stopping the flow. It had formed a nice little lake and they had built a mud hut in the center.

"I'll have to do something about this," he told the horse. "Dynamite will fix the problem. A hole in that dam will let the water out. But the beavers will still be here. I need to eliminate the beavers, but how? A shotgun would work, but I'd have to be here night and day to use it. Maybe I need to call the forest service and have the beavers removed and transplanted somewhere else. I'll go to town and talk to them and maybe get some dynamite to boot. I'll also look at the flyers at the sale barn and find a bull sale where I can get a bull."

Satisfied that he knew how to solve the problem, Mud decided to go to town the next day. The problem needed to be solved as soon as possible or he wouldn't have a garden growing for his next winter's food supply.

The next day he went to town and stopped at the hardware store. He noticed the same clerk that had helped him when he bought the fencing supplies. Deciding the clerk wouldn't be much help, he asked for the owner of the store, Mister Peters.

When Peters arrived, Mud said, "I need some dynamite. You got any?"

"What are you going to do Mud, take off your other leg?" Peters was trying to be funny, but Mud didn't see much humor in his statement.

"Nope," answered Mud. "I got some homesteaders on the property and need to move them out. They're stealing my water."

"I can't sell you any dynamite to blow up people. It's against the law," said Peters.

"Not people," replied Mud. "Beavers."

"Oh. That's different! I've got some. How much do you need?"

"Enough to blow up their dam and lodge."

"Half a dozen sticks ought to be enough," said Peters.

"But you should check with the fish and game department. It might be illegal to destroy beavers."

"They're doing me wrong and I need to get rid of them, but I'll check with the fish and game."

"I'll give you some extra fuse. You'll need to be quite a ways away when it goes off. You'll need some extra time to get away with that bum leg. This is a slow-burning fuse."

"Yeah, good idea," replied Mud.

Peters went to the back room and returned with six sticks of dynamite. "Keep this and the fuse dry at all times. It doesn't work when it's wet. I've given you extra length of fuse. It's a slow-burning fuse, so make sure you give it plenty of time."

When Mud left the hardware store, he went to the fish and game office. He explained his problem to the man in charge and asked if they could remove the beavers.

The game warden said, "We'd be glad to trap the beavers and transplant them but we can't start on it for two days. Then it might take a couple of days to get them all."

"I could probably do the job in about an hour," said Mud. "The dam has to come out anyway so I can water my garden and provide water for my livestock."

"Two days is the earliest we can get to it," said the warden. "We'd really like to put the beavers elsewhere. There's not many in this part of the country and we could certainly use more."

"I've already got the dynamite," said Mud.

"Have you ever used dynamite before?" asked the warden. "Do you know how to use it?"

"No on both counts," replied Mud. "I figured I'd set it, light the fuse and get out of the way."

"You better let us come out, trap the beavers and blow the dam. We have a man qualified to do that sort of thing. How do we get to your place?" asked the warden.

Mud gave him directions to the ranch and the warden wrote them down.

"I'll give these to our man. He'll be out there, early in the morning, in two days."

Mud left town and went to the sale barn. He noticed the sale dates for the upcoming bull sales and wrote them down. He wouldn't be able to go to any bull sales until after the beaver problem was solved.

He drove back to the ranch, not entirely happy that he had to wait two days before any action was taken on this project. Patience was not one of his virtues. But he had the dynamite and if the fish and game guys didn't get the job done, he figured he could.

He spent the next two days riding around the ranch, checking his cows. The second day he rode the mustang mare that had bucked him off. She didn't give him any trouble and actually acted like she liked to be ridden. When he got back to the ranch, he was surprised that the fish and game people hadn't shown up.

Just like the government, he thought, *tell you one thing and do another.*

The next morning, as he was making coffee, he heard a couple of vehicles approaching. Looking out the window he saw two fish and game trucks parking in front of the house. The occupants got out and he recognized one of them. It was Fred Wilson, Bud Wilson's brother. Mud only knew Fred casually, he'd spent his younger days running around with Bud. But he'd met Fred often enough to know him.

Mud met the fish and game people at the door. "Come in and get some coffee. If you got your own cups, better bring 'em. I only got two."

Fred entered the cabin first and shook hands with Mud. "I'm Fred Wilson, and you're Muddy Waters."

"That's right," replied Mud. "I recognize you from my earlier days with your brother Bud."

"I thought I knew the name," said Fred. "How have you been?"

"I've been getting along pretty good," answered Mud, as he poured coffee. "Got this little spread, a little bunch of cows, and few horses. Just about everything I need. I really can't complain. I did go up to Bud's last fall to help him with his cow gather, but I'm afraid I wasn't much help. It's been a long time since I've seen you, how have you been?"

"I heard you were at Bud's, and everyone there was glad you showed up," said Fred. "I've been okay. Getting ready to retire from the department. I've been with the department about thirty years or so. I'm ready to retire. We were supposed to be here yesterday, but I had to testify in court regarding some poachers we caught last fall and I'm the only one qualified to use dynamite that was close enough to get here. Just what's the problem?"

"Beavers have stopped the water flow to my garden and to a stock watering pond farther down the creek," answered Mud. "I need the garden and my stock needs the water. How come you brought so many people? I figured this was a one-man job. I could do it myself, I've got the dynamite."

"These guys, Bill, Wilber, and Ron, are fairly new to the department. The head of the department thought we could do some additional training with this little project."

"Well, I can't really put you up, I'm running a little short of groceries."

"We came prepared to camp. Can we camp here?"

"Sure," answered Mud. "Just be careful with your cooking fire!"

Fred laughed. "That's what *we* tell everyone! Just where is this beaver dam located? Can we get there in the trucks?"

"It'll be rough going, but you can get fairly close. After we finish this coffee, I'll saddle a horse and lead you there."

When everyone had their fill of coffee, Mud went out, saddled the horse Pat had given him and led the rangers to the beaver dam. It was slow going, and although Mud got a little irritated at how slow the trucks had to go, he was content that his water problem was soon to be alleviated.

They arrived at the dam. "This is it," said Mud, as the rangers got out of the trucks. You can see one of the beavers swimming across the little lake. It looks like he's draggin' an aspen branch."

"We'll survey the situation for a little bit," said Fred. "Wilbur, you're the trapper. You figure out where you want the traps. Bill and Ron, you can unload the traps and equipment. I'll look around and see if we can find a place to camp closer than Mud's. We'd spend too much time getting here every day to get much done."

"Don't pick a spot too close to the dam," said Wilbur. "We don't want to disturb the beavers too much. They'll be wary with the traps in place."

"You guys let me know when you're going to blow the dam. I'd like to see it," said Mud. "Right now, I've got other things to do."

"When we're sure we've captured all the beavers, we'll let you know," said Fred.

"By the way, what happened to the poachers?" asked Mud.

"One of them was a repeat offender. He got a pretty stiff fine, some jail time and the loss of his hunting privileges the rest of his life. The others were first time offenders, they lost their hunting privileges for five years and fines. The courts are getting stricter with regards to poaching. You don't go out and get a little red meat occasionally, do you Mud?" Fred was smiling as he asked the question. The seasoned old ranger had caught more than one poacher by asking the seemingly innocent question.

Mud was ready. He knew some of the tricks the ranger used. "Nope," replied Mud, although his answer wasn't entirely truthful. "I can raise better-tasting meat at home, although that renegade bull Pat shot last year was kinda tough. I get a license every year and get a spike buck just to vary the menu."

"That's good," said Fred.

Mud turned his horse to leave and said, "Don't forget to let me know when you're going to blast. I sure want to see it."

Fred nodded his head and started to look for a more suitable place for his crew to camp.

As Mud rode away, he thought to himself, *I really don't have much to do, but there isn't anything I can do here. And it will be nice if they find a place to camp rather than my front yard. I just don't feel comfortable with a lot of people around. I guess I can go mess with the mustang colt some.*

That night, the fish and game wardens hadn't returned and Mud thought they'd found a place to camp. He was satisfied.

The next few days, Mud just puttered around the ranch. He stayed pretty close, he didn't want to miss Fred coming by to tell him when they were going to blow the dam. After four days, he saddled a horse and rode to the dam. He found where the wardens had set up their camp and rode in. It looked like a comfortable camp. He was surprised to see only three of the rangers in camp.

"Where's the other one?" he asked. He didn't remember their names.

"He's went to town with the beavers we've caught," said Fred. "We figure we've only got to catch one more and we'll be ready to blow the dam and lodge. Ron will be back tonight."

"When do you figure on catching the other beaver?" asked Mud.

"Don't know," replied Fred. "They've become pretty wary. We've reset the traps and changed their position."

"Don't blow the dam unless you let me know," said Mud.

"Don't worry. As soon as we can, we'll let you know. I've got other things to do, even though we're enjoying this little official camping vacation. We need to get back."

Later the afternoon, Fred came driving up to the house. Mud saw him coming and stepped out on the porch to greet him. "You're here earlier than I figured."

"We're going to blow the dam in the morning," said Fred. "If you want to watch, you better be there about eight. We'll blow the dam, then when the water has drained, I'll walk out to the lodge and blow it. We'll bust a hole in the lodge and check just to make sure there aren't any beavers left. Then we can leave."

"You don't have to leave," said Mud. "You haven't been any bother to me."

"We need to get back to take care of other chores," replied Fred. "The taxpayers might get upset if they knew we were taking a vacation at their expense. That's what this actually has amounted to. While the taxpayers might get upset, if the beavers knew what was going to happen, they'd be grateful we took the time to relocate them."

Mud was up early the next morning and rode out to the ranger's camp. He was anxious to get his garden going and needed water to do it. He tied his mustang mare to a tree and walked into the camp.

"Need some coffee?" one of the rangers asked. He was starting to break camp.

Mud couldn't remember the ranger's name. "Nope," replied Mud. "I've already had plenty. When are you going to blow the dam?"

"Fred's out setting the dynamite now. Seeing as you're here, we can blow it anytime."

"Good. I'm ready. I'll ride over and watch."

"You might want to walk. That dynamite will make a pretty big noise and probably spook your horse."

It occurred to Mud that this ranger may have a lot of horse experience. "You're right," he said. "I'll walk. It's a longer walk home than over to the dam. I'll start now, I don't walk so well."

Mud met Fred as he walked to the dam.

"Are you ready to watch?" asked Fred. "I've set the dynamite. I set it right on top of the creek bed where the water used to run. We're set."

"I'm ready," answered Mud.

"I'll go get Wilbur. He'll want to inspect the lodge before we blow it. I'll be right back."

Mud continued to walk toward the dam. Presently, the rangers returned. Fred took up his position by the plunger and was ready to set the dynamite off. Looking around to make sure everyone was clear, he pushed the handle down.

Within a second, there was a big explosion and a loud bang. There was a loud rustling of the brush off to the west of the pond and a small herd of deer hurriedly ran off.

Water poured out of the opening in the dam filling the dry creek bed. It looked like a small flood.

"It's a good thing I haven't opened the ditch. My garden could have been flooded out," said Mud.

It wasn't long before the pond had been drained. The rangers put on rubber hip boots and walked out to the lodge with shovels and axes. Mud watched as they chopped and dug a hole in the top of the lodge. When they had a hole big enough, Wilber entered and soon came up again.

"Nothing in there," he said. "The place stinks. Smells like a bunch of rodents lived in there." He laughed at his own joke.

Fred set more dynamite around the lodge, set the fuse and they all moved to safety to blow the lodge.

He attached the fuse to the plunger and blew the lodge. All that remained of the dam was a hole and some broken tree limbs. Water that had been flowing into the dam continued to flow and found its way to the hole where the lodge had been. When the hole was filled, the water ran out to the old creek bed.

"That job's done," said Fred. "We'll load up and pull out. I'll be over at Bud's in a couple of weeks. Anything you want me to tell them?"

"You can tell Bud, Pat, Honey, and Sally, and of course Jimmy, I said hello, if you want," replied Mud.

"What about Virginia?"

"I don't have anything to say to her," said Mud.

"Oh? I thought you two used to be pretty thick," said Fred.

"That was a long time ago. It's been over and done for years," said Mud. "Just don't tell her where I am. I don't need to see her."

"Whatever you say," said Fred. "We'll be leaving as soon as we've packed up everything. We won't be going out by your house, we found an old road we can use to get to the main road quicker."

"I just brought you overland because it was closer than that old road," said Mud.

"Those deer that were spooked when we set off the dynamite, you haven't been keeping them around for other purposes, have you?" asked Fred.

"Certainly not!" replied Mud indignantly. "I didn't even know they were here. Had I known, I probably would have shot one and invited you to have supper with your own meat!"

Fred laughed. "I'll remember that."

The two men shook hands and Mud walked to where his mare was tied. "Looks like the noise really spooked you from the way the ground is chewed up," Mud told the mare. "Are you going to give me trouble on the way home?"

Mud untracked the mare and while he sensed the mare was a little nervous, she didn't give him any trouble on the way back to the ranch house. As he rode, he thought to himself, *I can start my garden now. I've got water.*

11

A New Bull

Mud now had water going down the creek. He could start planting his garden and irrigate it as needed. He looked forward to a fairly peaceful summer—tending his garden during the morning hours, riding out to check his cattle during the afternoon.

When Mud got back to the house, he checked the sale dates for the bull sale. Noticing a sale date only two days away, he decided to go to it. It would be a day's drive away, but he thought he could make the drive, get a room at a hotel in town, get a haircut, a shower and some new clothes and hopefully get a new bull.

The next day, he loaded the stock rack in the pickup and prepared to go to town. Before he left, he put his branding irons in the truck. If he got a bull, he'd brand him at the sale facility before he brought him home. He didn't have a chute and he wanted the bull to be carrying his brand when he turned him loose. He'd had a tough time branding the cows that Gene Fisher had given him without a chute, having to rope them, tie them down and get them branded. He didn't want to go through that again, not with an artificial leg hindering him.

He didn't have much trouble branding the calves. When

it came time to brand, he gathered his cattle and corralled them. He could rope the calves, tie them down and do the branding, earmarking, castrating, and vaccinating by himself. It was tough with the artificial leg, but he could handle it.

The next day, he turned his horses out on pasture. He drove to the town close to where the bull sale was being held and got a room in the hotel. Then he went to the western wear store and got some new clothes. He debated on whether or not to go back to the room and get a shower and change into the new clothes right away. He was still thinking about it when he went to the barbershop for a haircut. Not being one accustomed to changing clothes in the middle of the day, after his haircut he decided to go to the sale facility to see if he could use their cute to brand a bull if he bought one.

The managers of the sale facility were busy showing off their bulls for sale. Mud entered a group of people that were being escorted around and being told of each bull's lineage by a sale manager. Mud wasn't particularly interested in the lineage, he wanted a bull that would produce big healthy calves at weaning time. It looked like to him that these bulls were being shown off for purebred operators.

When the tour was over, Mud approached one of the managers and asked, "Is there any chance I could use your chute to brand a bull if I bought one here? I don't have one at my place."

"Sure," replied the manager. "What are you looking for?"

"I've got a cow-calf operation. I'm not interested in raising purebred, registered animals. But I need a bull that will throw calves that are easy to calve, yet grow out to be big-framed large weaners."

"As you probably know," said the manager, "these Angus bulls generally throw smaller calves, making calving easier. But the calves grow out to be nice, big-framed animals."

"I'm aware of that," replied Mud. "My operation is somewhat spread out and the cows need to calve out on their own. That's why I need an Angus bull."

"Certainly. I can show you a number of bulls that have the genetic capability to throw smaller calves. You can write down their sale numbers then bid on them when they come through."

"That will work," said Mud.

The sale manager took out his sale catalog and started pointing out bulls that would throw smaller calves. He got to one bull and said, "This bull is a three-year-old. We generally sell our bulls as two-year-olds, but he was a late calf and didn't have the size of the other bulls last year. We decided to hold him over and sell him this year. He should throw some smaller calves. He might be a good prospect for you. He's ready to go to work. As you can see, he's got the size now."

"I'll keep him in mind," said Mud, as he was impressed with the bull. He then returned to the hotel.

He got a good, long hot shower that night and then the next day, dressed in his new clothes, he went to the bull sale. He felt like a dude in his new clothes. The only thing he had on that wasn't new was his old hat.

He watched the sale as it progressed but didn't bid on anything. He was impressed with the three-year-old bull he'd seen the day before and decided if he was going to buy anything, it would be him. When the bull came through, the bidding started a little higher than he'd hoped, but he got in. He ended up buying the bull, but he thought he'd paid too much for him. He'd find out for sure next year when he sold the calves.

When the sale was over, he asked about branding the bull.

"We can do that right now, if you've got your irons."

"They're in the truck," said Mud. "I'll get them."

"I'll put your bull in the chute. You'd probably better pay for him before we brand him," said the manager, smiling.

"Yeah," said Mud. "That would be a good idea. If we branded him before he was paid for, I might not have to pay for him!"

They both laughed and Mud went to the office and paid for the bull. Then he went to the truck, got his irons and went to the chute. The sale manager hadn't put the bull in the squeeze chute. "We'll get the irons hot first then catch him," he said.

While they were waiting for the irons to heat up, Mud asked the manager, "Can I leave him here overnight, on feed and water and take him home in the morning?"

"Sure," replied the manager. "We can haul him to your place if you want, for an extra delivery charge."

"What's your delivery charge?"

"Two dollars a loaded mile," replied the manager.

"I'll get him home," said Mud. "I've got to go there anyways. I'll be here early in the mornin' to get him."

"How early?" asked the manager.

"About sunup," replied Mud.

The irons got hot and Mud branded the bull. Then he went to the brand inspector and got a brand inspection on the bull. Even though the bull had his brand, he needed the papers to show proof of ownership.

Mud went to the hotel, had a good steak dinner, spent some time watching television and went to bed. He thought it had been a good day and was satisfied.

The next day, at sunrise, he loaded the bull and started home. It was a long, slow trip. The bull was a little restless and periodically turned around. He was big enough that when he turned around in the stock rack, his movements caused the truck to swerve on the highway. The way he was weaving around, Mud thought he might get pulled over for drunk driving! Consequently, he had to drive slower. He found himself wishing he had taken the sale manager's offer to deliver the bull.

He arrived at his place later that afternoon, drove out to where he saw some of his cows, close to water, and unloaded the bull. His job for that day was done. Contented that he had accomplished something worthwhile that day, he went to house, fixed himself some supper, and went to bed early.

He spent the next few days putting in his garden. Then he went to the creek and turned water into the ditch. The water carried some debris down the ditch and Mud cleared it as he followed the water down to the garden. He already had his rows dug and when the water reached the end of the garden row, he'd go to the head of the row, shut the water off on that row and turn it into another. In a week or so he'd let the water run until each space between the rows was wet. He wasn't sure this was the right way to go, but somebody had told him it was the proper way to do it. He'd have to irrigate about once a week.

He kind of enjoyed taking care of his garden. He had plenty of water and often thought of himself as a little kid playing in the water. It made him happy.

12

Back at the Wilson Ranch

At the Wilson Ranch, after Mud had made his getaway, Virginia Abercrombie was quite upset. She missed her former flame and although she had tried to smooth things over by using every technique she could think of—from being very domineering, bossy, and assertive to being very coy, bashful, and charming. None of her actions had any effect on Mud. He tried to stay as far away from her as he could and he never initiated any conversation—all the conversation between them was started by Virginia. Mud had only replied to her as a matter of courtesy.

One day, a few weeks after Mud had left and she was beginning to return to her normal self, a letter arrived. It only had a post office box for a return address and the town was quite a ways from the ranch. It was addressed to Bud Wilson. Virginia had picked up the mail that day and noticed the letter, but didn't pay any attention to it. She handed the mail to Bud.

As Bud glanced through the mail, he saw the letter. "I wonder what this could be?" he asked as he opened it. "It's too early to be getting reservations and deposits for next summer. Why, it's from Mud!" exclaimed Bud. He quickly read through the short note.

Virginia turned quickly when she heard Mud's name,

and immediately regained her composure. She hoped no one had noticed. As nonchalantly as possible, she asked, "Oh? What does he have to say?"

Pat noticed how Virginia had acted at the mention of Mud's name, but didn't say anything. Pat didn't miss much.

"It's just a note to thank us for letting him help with the gather and a thanks for the money I sent him via Pat. That's it. He never was much good with words. But he hasn't forgotten his manners. It's good to hear from him."

"That's just like him," said Virginia. "Right to the point and no fussing around. I'll bet he doesn't even say how he's getting along. Let me see that."

Bud handed the letter and envelope to her. "I didn't hold anything back Virginia, all he said was essentially 'thanks.'"

Virginia took the letter and envelope and carefully read the letter. She then returned the letter to Bud, but not before taking a good look at the return address. She then went to her room and wrote the address down so she wouldn't forget it. No, she wouldn't send Mud a letter, but at some time in the future she might have to visit that town.

"I'd like to see that letter," said Pat.

Bud handed him the letter.

Pat read the letter. "I'd like to see the envelope also."

Pat took the envelope and made a note in his tally book about the return address and returned the envelope to Bud.

"What's that for?" asked Bud.

"I think I might want to send Mud a letter," replied Pat.

That night he composed a short note to Mud, put it in an envelope and gave it to Sally. "Would you kindly mail this next time you go to town? It's kinda important."

"Sure," replied Sally.

"I'd appreciate it if you didn't let Virginia see it, or say anything to her about it."

Sally gave Pat a funny look, but didn't say anything.

After seeing the envelope and committing the address to paper, Virginia's spirits improved considerably. Where before she had been coming out of a depression, she was now looking forward to each day. Everyone at the ranch noticed this and other than a casual, "You must be feeling good today," nobody said anything.

Things at the Wilson Ranch returned to normal with Virginia feeling better. She even seemed to be looking forward to the approaching winter. She was even looking forward to spending the winter in town with Sally, Ginny, and Bud. This was a drastic change, as she didn't think much of town. A transplant from town to the ranch, she really appreciated the ranch life. She had become enamored to ranch life earlier when she and Mud were engaged, but had been hustled off to town when she married Mister Abercrombie. That was a sudden, unexpected move and it wasn't until a few years later, after her husband had died, that she came to the Wilson Ranch. She had spent every summer there until Sally graduated from an exclusive private school. Then she moved to the Wilson Ranch on a permanent basis.

As the winter passed, Virginia became more excited. Sally noticed this and said, "Looking forward to going back to the ranch for the summer?"

"Certainly! Aren't you?"

"Of course. But this year, you seem to be more anxious about it. As a matter of fact, you've been in good spirits all winter. What's up?"

"Nothing," replied Virginia. "Spring is such a happy time of year."

Sally let it go at that, but suspected something else was going on.

13

Mud's Surprise

One day, around noon, Mud returned from his garden to find a strange car parked in front of the house.

"I wonder who that could be and what they want?" he said to himself.

As he rounded the corner of the house, he was surprised to see Virginia sitting on the porch.

"Dusty!" exclaimed Virginia when she saw him. She almost threw herself off the porch at him.

Mud was surprised and caught her, more out of surprise and self-defense.

"What are you doing here?" he asked.

"I needed to talk to you," replied Virginia.

"Who told you I was here? Pat? Fred? How did you find me?" Mud recalled Pat's letter and now he knew what Pat meant when he wrote, "Look Out!" Unceremoniously, he took Virginia's arms from around his shoulders.

"Nobody told me where you were," replied Virginia. "I saw the return address on your thank you letter and went to the post office in town. They couldn't tell me how to get here so I went to the sale barn and got directions to your place. Luckily, I found you."

"Unlucky for me," muttered Mud.

"But I need to talk to you, Dusty."

"Say what you've got to say, then you can go," said Mud.

"Dusty, I hurt you terribly in the past and I'm here to apologize and make whatever amends I can. I just don't know how to do it."

"Consider it done," replied Mud, thinking it was over. But it wasn't.

"For the last thirty or so years I've been living a miserable life over what I did to you," said Virginia. "And I've spent a lot of time trying to figure out what I'd do if I ever saw you again. I haven't come up with anything that I thought would be suitable."

"Nothing would be suitable," replied Mud. "Years ago, you did hurt me pretty bad. But you've done all right for yourself. You've got enough money to last you the rest of your life. Certainly more than I could ever have provided you with."

"Money isn't everything," Virginia said. "You must have come into some money to get this place. By the way, it's lovely."

"I didn't buy it," said Mud. "It was given to me."

"Given to you! Who would have given this lovely place to you?"

"Gene and Nancy Fisher gave it to me, free and clear. I guess I did 'em some favors and they paid me back, although they didn't have to. They were killed in a car wreck a few years ago, but they had already deeded this section to me. It's been mine for a number of years. They were as fine a folks that ever lived, as fine as Bud Wilson. How is Bud and everyone up there?"

"They're good. They don't know I've come down here. I just told them I had some things to do in town and would be gone a few days."

"Well, you can go back now," said Mud. "Then they won't worry. There's nothing you can do here."

"Dusty Waters! You're the most stubborn man I know! Are you still holding a grudge?"

"Yep."

"Why can't you let bygones be bygones?"

"It ain't in the cards. Now if you'll let me in my house, I'll fix some dinner before I have to check my cows. If you care to, I'll fix you something to eat before you go."

Virginia slowly moved to one side and Mud entered his house. Without being invited, Virginia followed.

"This place could certainly use a woman's touch," she said as she surveyed the place. Without asking or being invited, she started to wash the dishes that had accumulated in the sink.

Mud noticed this and said, "I'll take care of that."

"This is woman's work," replied Virginia. "Besides that, when I get done I'll know they're clean."

Mud didn't say anything and went to fixing his noon meal. Presently, they sat down to eat. The meal was eaten in silence, although Virginia tried to make conversation. Mud was noncommittal, although he was visibly nervous.

When they were done, Mud put his dishes in the sink. "I'll take care of 'em tonight, when I get done with chores. I suppose you'll be goin' and I suppose it was nice of you to visit. I need to saddle a horse and check my cows."

"Can't I go with you?" asked Virginia. "I used to ride with you quite often, years ago."

"That *was* years ago. Besides that I don't have a horse suitable for you to ride. And I don't have an extra saddle."

Mud went to the barn and caught the horse Pat had given him, saddled him and started out. As he rode by the house, he politely tipped his hat to Virginia, who was sitting on the porch. He rode off without looking back, until he reached the top of a hill. Then he looked back expecting to see Virginia's car gone. It wasn't.

He rode out of sight of the house and said to his horse, "I sure hope she's gone when we get done. I can't see any sense in her hangin' around, it sure can't result in any good."

Mud rode around and checked all his cows. He took a lot longer than necessary. He wanted to give Virginia plenty of time to leave. He didn't know what he'd do if she wanted to stay overnight.

While checking his cows, ne noticed a cow with a slight limp. "Probably some foot rot," he told his horse. "I didn't bring any medicine. Guess I'll have to come out tomorrow to rope her and give her a shot."

Long after he should have been back, Mud rode back to the ranch. He came from a different direction and couldn't see Virginia's car until he rounded the corner of the house. She was still there! She hadn't left!

Discouraged, Mud rode to the barn, unsaddled his horse, and gave him an extra measure of grain. He waited until the horse finished the grain, then went slowly to the house. In his mind he was trying to figure out what to say to get Virginia to leave. This was becoming a very uncomfortable situation for him.

As he entered the house, Virginia greeted him cheerfully. "Everything all right with your cows?" she asked.

"No." was Mud's curt reply. He noticed that the house had been cleaned and was a little surprised.

"What's the problem with your cows?" queried Virginia.

"Foot rot." Mud was not encouraging any conversation. "I thought you were leaving."

"I took a nap and when I woke up it was too late to leave so I fixed your supper," she replied. "While it was cooking, I cleaned the house. Doesn't it look nice?"

Mud didn't answer the question, but replied with one of his own. "What's for supper?"

"You have plenty of leftovers, all beef, but I wanted to fix you something different, so I got some frozen chicken out of the car. Supper is fried chicken."

"That will be different," said Mud.

"It's ready now. Wash up and we'll eat."

Wash up? thought Mud. *Why? I haven't even gotten dirty yet.* But he did go to the sink and ran some water over his hands.

"Don't forget to use soap!" reminded Virginia.

I'm being treated like a five-year-old child, he thought. *And in my own house!* But he did use soap.

"There," he said, turning around and holding out his hands for Virginia to see. "Does that look any better?" He couldn't see any difference.

"Yes," said Virginia, taking his hands in hers. "Much better!" She led him over to the table, still holding his hands. He tried to get loose, but Virginia had a firm grip on him.

The table was set. "You sit here," she said. She turned to get the chicken.

"But I sit here, where I can look out the window," said

Mud, changing his seating position. He had to rearrange the plate, coffee cup, and utensils.

"That's fine," said Virginia. "You can sit next to me if you wish." Virginia was beaming with satisfaction as she said that.

Nervously, Mud sat down in his accustomed position. He wasn't liking how this was going at all. *I'm going to have to do something and do it quick,* he thought. *I'll have some words with her after supper. Right now, there's no use in ruining a good meal. As I recall, Virginia used to be a pretty good cook.*

Once again, Mud ate in silence. He did enjoy the fried chicken. Virginia tried to initiate conversation but Mud only answered with simple, non-committal words. He was busy eating, but also thinking what he should say to her to get her to leave. He decided he'd have to be pretty tough and not spare her feelings. He didn't want anything to do with her and would have to make that clear.

With supper finished, Mud was about to read her the riot act, but she started first. "How did you like supper?" she asked.

"It was good enough, I suppose," answered Mud.

"How would you like something different every night?"

Feeling like he was being set up, Mud answered, "I get along fine on beef."

"You need more variety in your food, for your own health," said Virginia.

"My health's good enough," replied Mud. "Just what are you driving at and why are you here, Virginia?"

"As I said earlier today, I hurt you terribly in the past. I'm here to make my apologies and amends. I want to make it right with you and I'm willing to do whatever it takes. I have plenty of money and the rest of my life. Actually, we have the rest of our lives."

Mud became visibly nervous as she said what she said. *I'm going to have to put a stop to this right away,* he thought.

"Virginia," he said, "I'm trying to be courteous to you, but you had better stop all your thoughts about us gettin' back together again. You hurt me pretty bad about thirty years ago and I'm certainly not goin' to give you another chance to do it again. When you left me for Abercrombie, I became very depressed and seriously considered suicide. I didn't do it, obviously, mostly because of Bud and Pat's antics. But I resolved to never become committed to another human being. I've lived up here alone for quite a few years, thanks to Gene Fisher, and have become quite comfortable livin' alone. In fact, I've become very uncomfortable with company around. If you want to do somethin' nice for me, leave."

"You're a hard man! And a bitter one, Dusty Waters!" exclaimed Virginia.

"I'm what my experience has made me," replied Mud, in defense of himself. "I would suggest, for your welfare and mine, that you leave."

"Dusty Waters, you carry a grudge a long time! You're not a very forgiving man!"

"You're probably right," replied Mud. "However, I'm too old to change now. And why change? I'm happy here with who and what I am."

"But you could make other people happy!"

"Who and how?" asked Mud.

"Me, for one. By letting me make it up to you. By you

letting bygones be bygones. By us patching up the past and making a fresh start," pleaded Virginia.

"That won't work. I made up my mind years ago. I'm goin' to bed, I have a lot to do tomorrow. Hope you have a good trip back to the Wilson Ranch." Mud got up to leave and Virginia stood up.

"Dusty!" she pleaded.

"Good night!" was Mud's curt reply. He went to his bedroom and closed the door. As far as he was concerned, the conversation was over. He undressed, took off his artificial leg and got into bed. Presently, he heard the front door open and close and Virginia's car start and drive away. Soon he drifted off to sleep, content that he had solved the problem.

The next morning he was up early and drinking his coffee when he heard footsteps on the porch. "I wonder who that could be, this early in the morning," he said to himself. He was satisfied that Virginia had left. He went to the door, opened it and was totally surprised to see Virginia standing on the porch.

"I, ah ... thought you left last night," he stammered.

"I wasn't sure I could find my way back," said Virginia. "And I didn't want to leave you. I just moved the car last night."

"You need to leave and you need to leave now," replied Mud very sternly.

"You won't even offer an old friend a cup of coffee?"

"Well ... ah, yes. A cup of coffee," replied Mud. "But I'll guarantee you it won't do you any good to hang around. I've got to go find a cow and doctor her." Mud gulped down the last of his coffee and went to saddle his horse.

When his horse was saddled, he led him back to the house. He needed to get the penicillin to doctor the lame cow. Virginia was sitting on the porch, drinking her coffee.

She gave him a quizzical look.

"Forgot the medicine," said Mud, as he passed her and went into the house.

From the expression on her face when he returned, Mud thought Virginia may have thought he'd had a change of heart. *Fat chance,* thought Mud, as he got the penicillin.

Mud went right to his horse with the medicine without saying anything to Virginia.

"Hydrogen peroxide might be helpful treating that foot rot. Got any?" asked Virginia.

"Nope," was Mud's curt answer. "You'd best be gone when I get back." He got on his horse and rode away, without looking back.

As he rode, he asked his horse, "What are we goin' to do about that woman? If she's still there when we get back, I'll have to do something. Let's see, I've still got the dynamite I was goin' to use on the beavers. I could blow her to bits. But how would I do it? I wouldn't want to do it when she's in the house, I'd blow the house to bits. Besides that, she just cleaned it. Nope, that won't work. I could do it when she's in the car, but that would leave car parts and metal all over. The dynamite is out of the question. It would be murder. I'll have to think of something else."

Mud laughed at himself. He thought, *Am I really capable of murder? I don't know, but I do need to be rid of that woman.* After considerable thought, he concluded he couldn't murder Virginia, although it did bring him a strange pleasing thought.

"I'll have to think of something else," he told the horse. "Something legal."

After some more riding, he found the cow he was looking for. He roped her, choked her down, half-hitched the rope to the saddle horn, hobbled his horse and gave the cow a shot of penicillin. After the shot was administered, he took the rope from the saddle horn and took it off the cow. She didn't get up immediately, she was gasping for air.

As Mud was walking back to his horse, the cow finally got up. She ran over Mud, knocking him down. Luckily for Mud, when she knocked him down, she kept going. "That's a fine thanks I get for helping you out!" he yelled at the cow as he struggled to his feet.

He got to his horse, took off the hobbles, and got on. The cow hadn't hurt him when she knocked him down. "I think the female sex of all the different species on earth has it in for me!" he told his horse as they started out. "I'd best stay away from 'em all."

When he got back to the house, he rode around it before going to the barn. Virginia hadn't left yet, her car was still where she'd parked it the night before.

"I thought I'd made it clear that you weren't welcome here," he said as he entered the house. "When I left, I was actually thinking of ways to do you in, permanently, but couldn't come up with a legal one! I will go to the court and get a restraining order if I have to!"

"But Dusty ..."

"That's enough said!" exclaimed Mud. "Leave before I become violent!"

Virginia headed for the door and started to say something, but Mud cut her off. "Don't say anything else! The hurt was deep and it's healed now, but the scars are still present. Just leave!"

Virginia got to the door and turned toward Mud. Tears were running down her cheeks.

Mud noticed the tears and said, "Tears won't help! I've made up my mind. There's nothing more you can say! Just leave!"

Virginia left the house, not closing the door behind her. As she walked to her car, she slowly wiped the tears from her face. Halfway to her car she stopped, turned around and said, "You're a hard man Dusty Waters!" Without waiting for a reply she went to the car, got in and drove off.

Mud watched her go, satisfied that she was finally gone. Although he did feel a little guilty, he was glad to see her go.

He started to fix some supper and noticed a note on the table. It was from Virginia. Mud picked it up and read it.

Dear Dusty;

I didn't come up here to make you feel uncomfortable. I realized how badly I must have hurt you years ago. I only came to see if I could make things right with you. If there's anything I can do for you in the future, please let me know. I still have strong feelings for you. I just thought

The letter ended there. She didn't continue with her thoughts. It was signed, "Love Virginia."

"That's your problem, lady," said Mud, as if Virginia was still there. "You've been doin' too much thinking and not enough listening!"

Mud started his supper, feeling a little more guilty.

"Strange," he muttered, "I shouldn't feel guilty about kicking someone off my place that I didn't want here in the first place. I imagine I'll get over it soon enough."

The summer wore on and Mud stayed busy tending his garden and looking after his cows. Occasionally, when he was out riding and checking his cows, he thought about Virginia and wondered what she was doing.

Mud didn't have any more visitors during the summer and was quite content being alone. He would end up spending the rest of his life alone.

THE END

Other Books by Stu Campbell

Horsing Around a Lot

Horsing Around the Dudes

Humor Around Horses

You Can't Be Serious!

Comedy Around the Corral

More Humor Around Horses

A Young Cowboy's Adventure Series

A Young Cowboy's Adventure
Honey
Surprise!
Intruders
Expectations
Frozen
Advice
Broken
Ginny

Wild Horses for Wild Kids